DREAMS for COURAGE

Holiday Dreams Book 3

A Sweet Historical Western Romance

by

USA TODAY Bestselling Author

SHANNA HATFIELD

Wholesome Hearts
PUBLISHING

Dreams For Courage
Holiday Dreams Book 3

ISBN: 9798321714560

Shanna Hatfield
shanna@shannahatfield.com

Published by Wholesome Hearts Publishing, LLC.
wholesomeheartspublishing@gmail.com

Dedication

In memory of Doni

~*~

May we all find the courage
to pursue our dreams.

Books by Shanna Hatfield

FICTION

CONTEMPORARY

Holiday Brides
Valentine Bride
Summer Bride
Easter Bride
Lilac Bride
Lake Bride

Rodeo Romance
The Christmas Cowboy
Wrestling Christmas
Capturing Christmas
Barreling Through Christmas
Chasing Christmas
Racing Christmas
Keeping Christmas
Roping Christmas
Remembering Christmas
Savoring Christmas
Taming Christmas
Tricking Christmas

Grass Valley Cowboys
The Cowboy's Christmas Plan
The Cowboy's Spring Romance
The Cowboy's Summer Love
The Cowboy's Autumn Fall
The Cowboy's New Heart
The Cowboy's Last Goodbye

Summer Creek
Catching the Cowboy
Rescuing the Rancher
Protecting the Princess
Distracting the Deputy
Guiding the Grinch
Challenging the Chef

HISTORICAL

Pendleton Petticoats
Dacey *Bertie*
Aundy *Millie*
Caterina *Dally*
Ilsa *Quinn*
Marnie *Evie*
Lacey *Sadie*

Baker City Brides
Crumpets and Cowpies
Thimbles and Thistles
Corsets and Cuffs
Bobbins and Boots
Lightning and Lawmen
Dumplings and Dynamite

Hearts of the War
Garden of Her Heart
Home of Her Heart
Dream of Her Heart

Hardman Holidays
The Christmas Bargain
The Christmas Token
The Christmas Calamity
The Christmas Vow
The Christmas Quandary
The Christmas Confection
The Christmas Melody
The Christmas Ring
The Christmas Wish
The Christmas Kiss

Holiday Express
Holiday Hope
Holiday Heart
Holiday Home
Holiday Love

Chapter One

March 1886
Chicago

Leaning heavily on a crooked stick that served as a cane, Rhetta Wallace took another shuffling step forward, adjusting the basket she carried higher on her arm. Soot streaked her cheeks, and frizzy gray hair peeked from beneath a tattered rag she'd tied on her head. With a pronounced hump in her back and eyes squinting against the bright morning light, she smiled at a stranger passing by, revealing the blackened hole where front teeth should have resided.

"Psst! Rhetta. Psst!"

Rhetta pretended not to hear anything as she neared an alley. With slow, measured steps, she backed herself up to an upturned keg and settled her girth on the makeshift seat.

"What is it, Lee?" she asked, barely moving her lips as she turned ever so slightly toward the dark shadows of the alley.

"There's a man at your office. He wouldn't leave and told me I had to come fetch you."

"Name?" Rhetta asked, taking a long straw from her basket and sticking it in her mouth, pretending to chew on it.

"Said he represents Senator Tomlinson."

Rhetta almost choked on the straw and spit it out. Without looking behind her, she stood. "I'll be there as soon as I can. Give him tea and cookies."

"Will do."

From experience, Rhetta knew Leland Turner, her assistant and unofficial ward, would disappear into the shadows and return quickly to her office.

Rhetta continued down the street, keeping a steady eye on the man she was following. He turned at the corner, walked a few blocks to a residential area, and knocked on the door of a small home in need of paint and repair.

The door swung open, and a lovely young woman launched herself into the man's arms. He kissed her soundly, lifted her in his arms, and continued kissing her as he walked into the house and toed the door shut behind him.

Rhetta sighed, disappointed she'd been correct in assuming the worst. The irate wife who hired Rhetta to see if her husband was the philandering lout she'd determined him to be was going to be even more livid by news of this recent encounter.

Three times in the past two weeks, Rhetta had trailed the man to bawdy houses. Four days ago, he'd had a suspicious meeting in the park with a woman who'd appeared half his age. Notes were passed, and Rhetta could only guess it was information about a liaison.

Like this one.

She wrote down the address of the house and a few key notes on a writing tablet she took from the basket she carried, then stepped behind the nearest building, removed the rag and wig from her head and the shawl that looked like a dog had chewed it beyond redemption, stuffing them into her basket. The tip of her tongue worked to loosen the gum stuck to her front teeth. She tossed the black, sticky wad to the ground and wiped her fingers on her skirt.

Casting away the stick she'd used for a cane, she rubbed her cheeks on her dress sleeve to remove the soot, then walked to the corner and hailed a hansom cab. At her dirty, worn attire, he demanded payment before he'd take her to her office.

"Fine," she said, slapping a coin onto his palm with a huff. Rhetta sat back on the leather seat of the conveyance and reviewed what little detail she knew about Senator Tomlinson. The man was from Cincinnati. She wondered how he'd acquired her name since she lived in Chicago and had all her life. Then again, she had a string of wealthy clients who were good at passing along her name in referrals.

Rhetta generally hated the cases they hired her to pursue, like the wife who wanted evidence of her husband's wandering ways. But Rhetta took those jobs and charged outrageous fees, which allowed her to take on cases that mattered for the poor and underprivileged who had no way to pay. At the end of the day, she felt one thing balanced the other, which allowed her to rest peacefully. Or as peacefully as a woman who has spent the past eleven years working as a private detective could.

"Thank you," Rhetta said with cool politeness when the driver stopped as she'd directed, around the corner from the front door of her second-floor office. She rented the space above a photographer's studio. The photographer happened to be her cousin, so she was watched over by James although he had learned to mind his own business and not raise his eyebrows too high when she traipsed by his windows wearing one of her outlandish costumes.

Most of the time if she was in costume, Rhetta used the stairs located in the alley and entered through her back door. In a rush, she hopped out of the cab and raced around the corner into the alley, then took the stairs two at a time.

Rhetta jammed her key into the lock on her back door and swung the portal open, stepping into the hallway. She went directly into her costume room and found Lee had left a steaming pitcher of water for her to use to wash up.

"Bless that boy," Rhetta whispered to herself as she scrubbed her hands and face, removed the pins holding her hair close to her scalp, and combed out her long brown tresses. As she looked in the mirror and quickly styled her wavy hair into a loose coil she fastened at the back of her head, she surveyed her features.

Except for her bright blue eyes, Rhetta didn't think there was anything remarkable or even very memorable about her appearance. Her nose wasn't too long or too short. Her face not too round or oblong. Her chin could be a little on the stubborn side, but she had lips that weren't too puffy or too thin.

Overall, she felt average, which worked well when she wanted to blend in with a crowd. Not quite as well for attracting a suitor although Rhetta was not looking.

Men found her too bold, opinionated, and determined for their liking. After the number of unfaithful husbands she'd been hired to follow, she wasn't convinced a faithful one existed among the male species.

With flying fingers, she unbuttoned the ragged dress, removed the padding she'd fastened around her middle, and tossed off a petticoat fashioned from an old bed sheet.

She yanked on a lace-trimmed petticoat, pulled on her skirt and shirtwaist, then added a jacket that gave her a polished, professional appearance. The pink ensemble, edged in black, was striking and elegant, and a gift from one of Rhetta's clients. In fact, Mrs. Brown had been most generous in giving Rhetta five expensive outfits the woman had no longer been able to wear after giving birth to twins two years ago.

Mr. Brown had been one of the exceptions to Rhetta's rule that all men were detestable brutes. She'd followed him almost daily for a month and discovered the reason he kept secrets from his wife was to plan a surprise party for her birthday. Once Rhetta relayed that happy news, the woman had been elated and paid Rhetta's fee with a bonus, as well as offering the clothes that Rhetta had been thrilled to receive.

With a slight tug to the hem of the jacket to adjust it, Rhetta touched a bit of her favorite perfume to both wrists. Regardless of her career, a woman needed to feel feminine, at least to Rhetta's way of thinking.

She breezed from the room and down the hallway toward the entry area, where Lee had his own desk. He kept anyone from storming any further into the office without his approval and was there to receive visitors.

Years ago, she'd been watching the sale of ill-gotten goods in a seedy neighborhood when she caught a little boy trying to pick her pocket. Rhetta had grabbed him by the seat of the pants when he'd started to run off and peppered him with enough questions he finally burst into tears and confessed he had no home and couldn't recall his parents or if he had any siblings. He'd been living on the streets as long as he could remember.

Rhetta had taken him home and fed him, cleaned him up, and given him a place to sleep. In the morning he'd been gone, but he'd returned a few days later, starving, and sporting a black eye. As he'd wolfed down a bowl of hearty beef stew, she'd made him a bargain. If he stayed, she'd keep him fed, give him a warm bed, and never hit him if he in turn agreed not to leave without telling her where he was heading, refrained from stealing from her, bathed with some regularity, and would work as her assistant.

He'd shaken her hand in agreement, and Lee had been with her since. Neither of them knew his birth date, so they chose the day she'd first encountered him as his birthday. Rhetta had guessed him to be around six when they met, and Lee had just turned fourteen two weeks ago.

As a private investigator, Rhetta had done everything she could to unearth Leland's identity and some record of his existence, but it was as if he'd fallen from the sky and landed in Chicago's slums.

Regardless, she had made inquiries about adopting him. It seemed a judge would rather a boy live homeless and alone than allow a single woman perfectly capable of providing a stable home to adopt him. So, despite the lack of legalities, Rhetta considered Lee her son. Likely the only one she'd ever have since she would turn twenty-nine in April.

According to the whispers she occasionally overheard from people who liked to gossip, she was an old maid too contrary and odd to ever catch a man.

Rhetta wasn't contrary or an old maid, at least to her way of thinking. Besides, she had no time for putting up with the demands of a husband when she had a boy who needed her and work that fulfilled her. The bit about her being odd … well, that was perhaps disputable. She had always felt different from the other girls her age. She'd never been content to sit at home sewing samplers. Not when her father had encouraged her to dream big dreams and follow an adventurous path.

Rhetta stepped into the reception area and glanced at the dour-faced man seated on a chair in the corner. She looked at Lee, and he shrugged. With a smile plastered on her face, she took a step toward the man, extending her hand in greeting. "Hello, Mister …"

"Reynolds," Lee whispered in her ear, handing her a fresh writing tablet and pencil.

The man ignored her outstretched hand, so she withdrew it.

"Welcome, Mr. Reynolds," she said, forcing herself to maintain a smile. "How may I be of service to you today?"

The man stood and gave her a long, narrowed-gaze study. "You kept me waiting long enough, Miss Wallace. However, Senator Tomlinson is determined to speak with you about a delicate matter."

Rhetta had no notion as to what *delicate matter* the senator wanted to discuss, but she had an idea it was one she wouldn't like. Was his wife still alive? She couldn't recall. Whatever he sought her assistance with would likely be something scandalous and ridiculous, but she'd take the case because she had several clients unable to pay who truly needed her assistance.

"Is the senator in town?" Rhetta asked, meeting the man's stare with a frosty glare of her own. She refused to be cowed by him, especially in her own office.

"No. He's willing to pay your travel expenses if you could meet him next Tuesday."

"I will meet with him, but I make no promises other than arriving on time."

"Very well." The man took a thick envelope from the pocket of his coat and handed it to her. "All the information you'll need for the trip is in there." He tipped his head to her and left without another word.

Rhetta sank onto an overstuffed chair and looked at Lee. He stretched his arms above his head, leaned back slightly, and then grabbed the lapels of the vest he wore as he lowered his voice. "I'm Mister Mighty Britches, come to toss out demands from a corrupt politician. You will listen and obey me, little woman."

A chuckle rolled out of her before she could rein it in. Lee was forever doing impersonations, most of them quite well, and making her laugh.

"Sit down, you rascal, and let's see what Senator Tomlinson has to say."

Rhetta opened the envelope to find two train tickets, reservations for two rooms at one of the city's finest hotels, and a map with details for meeting the senator at a park near the hotel. It seemed she was welcome to bring Lee if she chose. The fact that the senator knew about Lee bothered her. Had he hired someone to spy on them? Someone like Mr. Reynolds?

A shiver slid over her spine at the thought of anyone watching them. Despite her aversion to this case and the senator, she decided she'd at least hear him out.

It looked like she and Lee were about to go on a short journey.

"I get to go?" Lee asked, reading the note she passed to him.

"Yes, you do. We'll pack tomorrow after we return from the church service and lunch with the cousins. The tickets appear to be for the afternoon train Monday, but I'll see if we can switch to a morning departure. I want time to visit the park and get a better idea of the area where we'll be staying."

"What can I do to help?"

"Make sure my satchel is packed with fresh supplies. We'll need tablets, pencils, and contracts in the event I decide to take this case." She handed him the unused writing tablet and pencil. "You are in charge of bringing snacks."

Lee grinned. The past few months, he seemed to have two hollow legs. The only time he didn't complain about being hungry was when he was sleeping. Rhetta had always kept fruit and cookies at the office for him to snack on after school and on the weekends if he accompanied her there. Now, she had whole loaves of bread, dried strips of beef, and tins of crackers, as well as fruit and cookies.

Thankfully, there was a bakery across the street and a café just around the corner if he ate all of the food in the office before she could replenish it.

"I'll make sure we have plenty of snacks. Is there a trunk I can pack them in?"

Rhetta gave him a playful nudge, knowing he was teasing. She rose and gathered the contents of the envelope Mr. Reynolds had left, tucked them inside, then walked into her office.

She wrote a letter to the wife of the cheating husband, sealed it in an envelope, and sent Lee to deliver it, then made her way to the train depot to see about switching their tickets.

Although she dreaded meeting the senator, part of her was excited about embarking on a new adventure.

Chapter Two

"Just act naturally, and everything will be fine," Rhetta assured Lee as she straightened the tie he wore with a dark blue suit. He looked quite dashing, or as dashing as a gangly boy who'd recently had a growth spurt can appear. She'd purchased the suit for his birthday, and thankfully, he hadn't yet outgrown it. The pants were getting shorter by the day, though, and she'd have to let out the hem soon, but the jacket had room for him to grow before the sleeves turned impossibly short or the shoulders grew too tight.

"Are you sure about this, Rhetta?" Lee asked, glancing around them as they left the hotel lobby and walked the two blocks to the park where they were to meet Senator Tomlinson.

"I'm quite certain we will be safe in the park. However, in the event the meeting does not progress in the manner we anticipate, you know the quickest route to the police station. We walked there yesterday after dinner."

"I know, but why are you meeting at the park instead of his office? Doesn't he have an office here in Cincinnati?"

"He does, and those same questions have popped through my thoughts, but it may be that he is trying to keep this meeting a secret, although the park seems to be quite a public place if that were the case. At any rate, I'm sure all will be fine. Just stand in that spot behind the garden statue, like we discussed yesterday, and I'm sure all will be well. If you see me open my parasol, run and don't look back."

Lee nodded although Rhetta had her doubts he'd run if her life were in danger. He'd be more apt to take her parasol and attempt to harpoon someone with it. Perhaps she never should have asked her cousins to teach him how to defend himself. They'd done far too good of a job if Lee's scuffles at school were any indication. His inability to stay out of fights was the reason she'd pulled him out of school and decided to teach him herself. He'd learned more from her in the past two months than he had in the last two years at the public school he'd attended.

Soon, though, Rhetta feared he'd exceed her knowledge and ability to teach him. Perhaps, with another job or two like this one that paid exceedingly well, she could hire a private tutor for him. Lee would likely balk at the notion, but she wasn't giving him an opinion on the matter. Education was important to his future success.

Rhetta stopped across the street from the park and moved into the shadows of the building behind them. She fussed with Lee's collar, then gave him an encouraging smile.

"I'm going to walk through the park from this entrance," she motioned across the street with the lace parasol she carried. "You walk around to the other side and enter from the south. I'll be watching for you, Lee. Be careful." Rhetta waited until he'd crossed the street and disappeared around the corner before she walked into the park and made her way to the bench where she'd been told to wait for the senator.

Rhetta arrived at the bench, located near a fountain in a secluded area. Surrounded by trees and shrubs, the bench was shielded from view by any passerby. It was almost like a secret garden, if the winding path to reach it was any indication. The area was quite lovely, though. The whole park was, with trees budding and flowers hinting they would soon be in bloom.

Had circumstances been different, she would have enjoyed exploring the park and the city, but she was here for business. If no delays arose, she and Lee planned to return home tomorrow.

Under the guise of brushing lint from the skirt of her pale green walking suit accented with raspberry trim, she looked around her, seeing three men stationed nearby, appearing prepared to guard someone or something. The way they carried themselves made her think they were likely on the senator's payroll.

Rhetta straightened her jacket, fluffed the lace at the collar of her raspberry shirtwaist, and adjusted her deep pink gloves. Would the senator find her outfit too … colorful? It was one of her favorite suits for meeting clients because it was expensive and perfectly tailored to her form, and the particular shade of deep pink—her favorite—gave her confidence.

With one more look around, Rhetta perched on the edge of the bench, using the parasol for balance. Bustles were such a botheration, even if they were the height of fashion.

As she waited for the senator's arrival, Rhetta wondered if women in the west wore bustles. Maybe they donned britches? Now there was a novel idea. The times Rhetta had donned pants for a costume, she'd so enjoyed the freedom of movement she'd experienced while wearing them, she'd almost hated to return to wearing a skirt.

She shifted slightly and saw Lee move into place behind the statue, hidden by it and the shrubbery around him. She nodded once to let him know she was aware of his presence, then set her gaze on the fountain. Sunbeams speared through the water, creating a dazzling display.

"It's lovely, isn't it?" a voice asked from above her. Rhetta had heard footsteps approaching but hadn't looked up until the voice spoke.

She turned and studied the face of an older, distinguished gentleman flanked by three burly men, all wearing gun belts with pistols at their hips.

Slowly, Rhetta stood. "It is lovely, Senator Tomlinson. The sunlight is much appreciated after the long days of winter."

"Spring has arrived earlier this year, thank goodness. I was ready for the winter to end by the second day of January," the man said, motioning for Rhetta to resume her seat on the bench. "Would Mr. Turner care to join us, or does he prefer to remain lurking in the shrubbery?"

Rhetta held up a hand, motioning with her fingers for Lee to come out from behind the statue. He walked over to them, removed his hat, and tipped his head with the politeness Rhetta had ingrained in him.

"It's a pleasure to meet you, sir," he said, addressing the older man.

"You as well, young Turner. If your …" The senator paused, as though he wasn't certain what to call Rhetta. "If Miss Wallace has no objection, one of my men would be happy to take you to the bakery across the street. They bake the best sugar cookies in town."

Lee gave Rhetta a hopeful glance, and she nodded. One of the big men took a step away, and Lee followed him, but not without looking back at her with a concerned glance.

"I'll be fine," she mouthed to him, and he nodded, then hurried to catch up to the senator's hired man.

"I hope all this," the senator waved his hand to encompass his guards as well as the park, "doesn't frighten you, Miss Wallace."

"It's only slightly off-putting, sir." Rhetta saw no reason to speak anything other than the truth.

Senator Tomlinson grinned, and she saw beyond the weathered lines on his face to the handsome man he must have once been. She supposed he still was, if one were interested in a man nearing his sixties. His hair was thick and full although it was streaked with silver. His eyes were gray and alert, rimmed with dark lashes. He appeared powerful despite his age and had a charismatic bearing she'd learned many politicians possessed.

"Do you always speak your mind, Miss Wallace?" the senator asked.

"Usually. I find it saves time and causes far less distress than trying to tiptoe around the truth."

"I admire that in a person," he said.

She wondered if part of that admiration came from her being someone out of the public eye who could speak her mind without worry of the adoring public catching wind of what had or hadn't been said.

"There must be a reason you asked me to meet you here, sir. I'd like to know why you sought out my services and how I may help."

The senator nodded, then looked around him. His hired men all moved back several paces. It was then Rhetta realized they were blocking off this section of the park so no one could enter, see who occupied it, or hear what was shared.

"If the matter is highly sensitive, might there be a better place to discuss the specifics?"

"We'll be quite undisturbed here. For all intents and purposes, if anyone saw me, they would assume I'm out for my daily walk around the park." The senator took a seat on the opposite end of the bench, then handed Rhetta a large envelope.

"You'll find most of the details in there." He glanced at the fountain, then back at her as she pulled out a folder stuffed full of information. "I'll tell you what I know. After you review all that," he tapped the folder, "if you have questions, you may send word through Mr. Reynolds, and we'll arrange to meet again. If you decide to pursue this case, you'll be adequately compensated. I'll also pay for all traveling expenses incurred for both you and your lad."

Rhetta nodded, not bothering to open the file before returning it to the envelope. She set it on her lap, removed a small writing tablet from her reticule along with a pencil, and prepared to take notes.

Senator Tomlinson seemed pleased she hadn't already bombarded him with a barrage of questions, but attentively waited to hear his story.

"My wife and I had only one child, Richard, whom we affectionally called Ricky. He was intelligent, kind, and occasionally prone to a bit of mischief, but no more than any other boy his age. When he was eight, a new boy began attending classes at his school. His name was Reed Saunders. Those two were as thick as thieves from the first day they met. Reed was about six months younger than my boy, but they were in the same grade. Liked many of the same things. Reed came from a terrible background. His mother was a working girl, and he'd been raised in a brothel. A truant officer insisted he be allowed to attend school, or he likely never would have set foot inside the schoolhouse. Eventually, one of his mother's clients died and left her everything. It included a small house and enough money that she could leave the brothel, although I don't think she quit her line of work. Anyway, when the boys were fifteen, Reed shot and killed my son, then disappeared without a trace. I've searched for him for twelve years. I almost caught up to him in Virginia, then again in Texas about six years ago, but I've lost him, Miss Wallace, and I want to find him. He needs to stand before a judge and God and be tried for the atrocious crime he committed in killing Ricky. That's all I want. Justice."

Rhetta thought the senator leaned more toward revenge but kept those thoughts to herself. "And your wife? Is she also adamant about finding Mr. Saunders?"

A pained look flashed across the man's face. "She died eight years ago."

"I'm so sorry, sir. What a terrible loss that must have been for you."

He nodded and cleared his throat. "When you find a missing person, what is your standard procedure of operation?"

"Depending on the case, I either contact my client or the authorities. In a case such as this, I would contact the nearest officer of the law, then send a telegram to you."

"That is what I wanted to hear." The senator leaned back and gave Rhetta an observant study.

"You are very good at what you do, Miss Wallace. Is that because of your own tragic background or your determination to be the best?"

"A bit of both, I suppose." Rhetta was unsettled by the fact that the senator had looked into her past. "Why did you seek me out, Senator? You could hire any number of private detectives. Why me?"

"Because I've heard your name come up over and over again as someone who completes the task set before you, and you do it with discretion. Those are two things not every private detective can boast."

"I don't boast, sir."

"I know you don't. I've had you followed and investigated, and I have more than a dozen referrals from people I trust, Miss Wallace. You are impeccable, and that is why I wish to hire you." He took a slip of paper from his pocket and slid it toward her on the bench. "I'll pay half of that figure now, and the rest once you find Mr. Saunders. If you discover he is deceased, a copy of his death certificate will suffice, and you will still receive the second installment of the payment."

"I will give the matter the consideration it is due and provide my response this evening. Would Mr. Reynolds be available to meet me in the hotel lobby at six?"

"That will be acceptable. I'll have Mr. Smith walk you over to the bakery and escort you and young Mr. Turner back to the hotel."

"Thank you, sir." Rhetta stood as did the senator. He politely tipped his head to her and gave her a look that held both sorrow and pleading. A part of her thought the senator could have been a talented actor had he decided to take to the stage.

She hadn't yet landed on his real reason for wanting to find Mr. Reed Saunders, but the case was certainly intriguing. She picked up the paper he'd slid toward her on the bench, tucked it and the tablet and pencil into her reticule, and gave the politician a polite nod before she started down a path that would lead to the bakery. One of the broad-chested men fell into step slightly behind her.

"Have you always lived in Cincinnati, Mr. Smith?"

The man made not a sound and continued staring straight ahead, making it clear he was not going to converse with her.

Rhetta swallowed a sigh. At the bakery, she collected Lee, who had a box full of pastries to take with him, and they walked to the hotel in silence with Mr. Smith's large form overshadowing them. He pushed open the lobby door, tipped his hat, then left.

"What was that about?" Lee asked as they made their way upstairs to their adjoining rooms on the second floor.

"I believe he was given orders not to speak with us. That's all. It's a common thing for men in his profession."

"Oh." Lee waited until Rhetta unlocked the door to her room to bound inside and set the pastries on the table. "The cookies were so good, Rhetta. Mr. Jones said I could choose as many as I like, so I got a dozen of them and cinnamon rolls for our breakfast and two berry tarts for dessert."

"Well, it sounds like you had quite a delicious visit to the bakery." Rhetta removed her pale green hat adorned with raspberry roses and ribbon that matched her ensemble, then shrugged out of the jacket that featured the bright pink hue on the lapel and the three buttons on each side of the waist.

"I like that dress. It's happy." Lee sprawled across the couch and opened the box from the bakery, taking out a cookie and biting into it.

"A happy dress?" Rhetta asked, amused.

"The colors are happy, and you always look happy when you wear it. It's a happy dress."

"I suppose it is, and I do." She walked over to the table in the corner, set down the envelope, and took a seat. The first thing she did was open the slip of paper the senator had given her with the wages he'd suggested.

"Oh, my gracious!" she whispered, pressing a hand to her chest. At first, she thought Senator Tomlinson had merely added one too many zeroes, but considering what he was asking her to do and the clients she wouldn't be able to take while she traveled in pursuit of Reed Saunders, the total didn't seem quite as exceedingly exorbitant.

Still, if she succeeded, she could afford to hire a good tutor for Lee and set aside funds for college. She could perhaps hire a real assistant instead of relying on Lee, who should be spending his time being a boy instead of working with her.

For no other reason than the financial benefits this would allow her to provide for Lee, she would take this job.

Now, she just had to figure out where to begin and what end the senator hoped to achieve when she found Mr. Saunders.

"Lee, would you be a dear and have the front desk send up a tea tray? Be sure to have them include milk and sandwiches for you." Rhetta called over her shoulder as she strode toward her bedroom. If she was going to work, she needed to be comfortable.

Quickly, she removed her shoes, changed out of her outfit into a serviceable dark blue skirt and blue and white striped shirtwaist, rolled the sleeves up to her elbows, and returned to the table to find Lee had returned.

"They'll send the tray up shortly," Lee said, taking two tablets and a handful of pencils from her satchel and sliding into the seat across from her at the table. "I'll help. Tell me what to do."

"Thank you, darling boy." Rhetta gave him an affectionate smile. "I'll have you start making a timeline once I get into the notes. For now, listen for the tea tray. I was too nervous to eat much earlier, and I'm famished."

Lee grinned. "Me too."

She laughed, knowing how much he'd eaten at both breakfast and lunch, not to mention at the bakery, and the four cookies he'd just devoured.

While he waited to answer the knock at the door with their tea tray, Rhetta dove into the notes the senator had provided. He had reports from a dozen private detectives from major cities throughout the east and south. There were sketches and drawings, all of the same man. Reed Saunders.

Lee set a cup of steaming tea and a plate of little sandwiches and cakes in front of her, then disappeared from her line of view. Absently, Rhetta sipped the tea, nibbled at the food, and wrote down notes.

She was nearly to the bottom of the file when she pulled out a photograph of two boys who looked so much alike, she would have thought them twins if the back of the photo hadn't stated their names as Ricky and Reed. She sat back in the chair, stunned by her discovery.

Reed Saunders wasn't just a random boy the senator's only child had befriended.

He was the senator's son.

A thousand questions roared through her head. Some of them the senator could have answered, but she doubted he would. The rest? Well, she had a feeling Reed Saunders would be the only one who could tell her the truth.

Had he really shot the person who was likely his half-brother? Had he known Senator Tomlinson was his father? Had Ricky known Reed was his brother?

Rhetta riffled through the papers, pulling out a photo of the senator with his wife and son. She compared it with the photograph of the two boys, stunned by the resemblance not only between the two boys, but between them and the senator. A single doubt did not exist in her mind that Richard Tomlinson had fathered both Reed and Ricky.

He'd said Reed was six months younger than his son. Had the senator, who wasn't a senator at the time but an aspiring politician, been visiting brothels while his wife was pregnant? And in those visits, had he produced a son with one of the harlots?

Why hadn't Senator Tomlinson been forthcoming with all the facts instead of what he wanted her to know? He had to have known she'd unearth the connection between him and Reed after looking through the file. Or did he assume no one was clever enough to piece the puzzle together?

Likely, there were many, many more secrets he kept hidden, but she wouldn't think about that at the moment.

Right now, she needed to decide if she could justify working for a man who was clearly a liar with questionable morals.

Rhetta had to reach a decision if the money she would receive from this case would be worth working for the conniving senator. Despite his lack of scruples and integrity, Rhetta felt a growing fascination to find the truth about this case, about what happened to a boy named Reed.

The first and most logical thing to do would be to find Reed's mother. The senator had mentioned she'd inherited a house from a client. Surely, there would be a record of that somewhere.

"Lee!" she called, then realized the boy had taken a seat at the table across from her as he ate his sandwiches.

He wiped his mouth on a napkin and gave her a curious look.

"I need you to inquire at the front desk about having someone change our train tickets. We won't be going home tomorrow. Ask them if we can change them to a Friday afternoon departure." She glanced over as he started to rise, then waggled her hand at him. "Finish your sandwiches and milk first."

Lee nodded, then bit into a second thick ham sandwich. She had no idea where he tucked away all that food, but she'd heard growing boys could eat a family out of house and home. Now that Lee was in the midst of a growth spurt, she believed it.

However, the funds from this case would alleviate any concerns about keeping food on the table for a good long while.

Before she could ask, Lee got up and refilled her teacup, stirring in a generous spoon of sugar, then returned to eating his sandwich.

By five that evening, the hair Rhetta had carefully styled for her meeting with the senator looked like birds might have nested in it. She had three pencils poking out of the lopsided knot, and paper cuts on two fingers that she'd wiped on her skirt. Good thing it was dark and wouldn't show the blood.

"Read the timeline to me again," she said, getting up from the table and pacing the room as Lee read through the progression of events as told to her by the senator, and mined from the notes she'd meticulously studied all afternoon.

"So, after Mr. Saunders shot Ricky Tomlinson, he fled. He turned up in New York City a year later, only to disappear again and not be seen for three years until he was spotted in Jamestown, Virginia. From there, he traveled to Kentucky, then

Tennessee and Texas, where his last known location was working on a ranch near Abilene."

"That's right." Lee sat back and set the writing tablet he held on the table. "He could be anywhere, couldn't he, Rhetta?"

"He certainly could be. The question is where?" She walked over and stared out the window, watching the busy street below. If she wasn't mistaken, she was sure one of the senator's hired men stood across the street, standing guard. Disturbed by his presence, she refused to show it. "Where would you go, if you were Reed Saunders and just wanted to be left alone?"

Lee grinned. "That's easy. I'd head west."

Rhetta spun around. "Of course. Where, though? California? Montana? Oregon?"

"I'd go to Oregon. I liked those stories you read to me about the Oregon Trail, when the pioneers first traveled it. I think it would be a wonderful place to live."

"You do?" Rhetta asked, blinking at the boy she'd known for eight years, but had never realized he was interested in Oregon. She'd never asked where he wanted to live or what he envisioned for his future. He'd always been so grateful to have a home with her, she might have taken a few things for granted. She assumed when he was of age, she would send him to college, and he'd pursue some worthwhile degree that would enable him to find a good job with good pay that would set him up to have a good life. Now, she realized how presumptuous and erroneous her thoughts were when it came to the boy she regarded as her son.

Lee nodded. “I read the articles in the newspaper about places in Oregon. There are towns in the mountains, and towns by rivers. Towns that are becoming cities. There are also lots of places where there are no people at all. Did you know there’s a place in the center of the state where the grass is as tall as a man’s head? It’s a land of opportunity and growth.”

She walked over and feathered her fingers through his hair, wondering when the little boy she’d come to love had grown up so much. A sudden fear she would blink and he’d be a man living on his own made her want to refuse to let him change or ever leave her, but she settled for giving him a hug. He hugged her back, then she kissed his forehead.

“If I accept this client and challenge, it will mean weeks if not months of travel. You’ll have to come with me. What do you think? Do you want to pursue this adventure or return home and forget we ever heard of Senator Tomlinson?”

“I get to vote?” Lee asked, looking completely taken aback with surprise widening his eyes. “You want my opinion?”

“I certainly do. This isn’t like any case I’ve taken on before, Lee. Typically, if I’m out of town on business, it is a night or two at most, and you stay with James and his family, but it could take considerable time and effort to unravel Mr. Saunders’ whereabouts. If you prefer I refuse this job and we return home, I will let Mr. Reynolds know the senator needs to find someone else to track down Mr. Saunders. Tell me what you want to do."

"Go! Let's go! I've never been to any of the places we just talked about, and I'd really, really like to see Oregon."

She smiled indulgently. "The trail might not lead us there, but it is a possibility. Do you truly want me to accept this job?"

"I do, Rhetta. I think Senator Tomlinson is a snake in fancy clothes, but it's important to find Mr. Saunders. If he's guilty, he should serve time for what's done. If he's innocent, then everyone should know the truth." Lee smiled while his eyes sparkled with the possibilities before them. "It will be like we're on a quest."

Rhetta hid a smile, knowing Lee had been quite taken with the knights of old in the stories he'd recently begun reading. "It will be like that."

Lee glanced at the clock and stood, pulling the pencils from her hair. "You'd better get ready to meet Mr. Reynolds. It's half past five."

"Goodness!" Rhetta raced into her room and rushed to fix her hair. She rolled down her sleeves, righted the buttons that were askew on her shirtwaist, slipped on a jacket that matched her skirt, and pinned on a plain blue hat. After gathering a pair of gloves, she returned to the table and took out two copies of her standard contract form that she'd brought with her. With a pen she dipped in an inkwell provided by the hotel, she filled in the details, signed her name and added the date, then quickly wrote a note with her stipulations for accepting the case. She folded the sheets of paper together, tucked them into an envelope, and snatched her reticule off the table by the door.

"Come along, Lee. After we meet Mr. Reynolds, we might as well enjoy dinner in the hotel's dining room. Make sure you slip on your jacket. We'd better smooth your hair." She reached out with her hand to guide the thick blond strands into place, while Lee ducked and dodged her attempts, making them both laugh.

"You have always been such a little rascal," she said, slipping her arm around his as they made their way down the stairs. "Don't ever change."

"I won't, Ma …"

Many times, Lee had come close to referring to her as his mother, but he'd not once come right out and said the words. She'd never wanted to push him, but it seemed far past time to address the issue.

Rhetta stopped at the base of the stairs and turned to face him. "Lee, you are welcome to call me Mom, or Mother, or whatever name you choose. Well …" she grinned at him, "any name within reason. If your preference is to continue to refer to me as Rhetta, that is also perfectly fine."

He returned her smile and nodded. "I know. I've thought of you as my mama for years, but you're so young, I didn't think you'd want me calling you that."

Tears stung her eyes and threatened to spill out, but she blinked them away. "I would love it if you did, darling boy." She gave him a one-armed hug, and then they continued to the lobby where Mr. Reynolds sat on a plush chair, reading a newspaper.

He rose at their approach, his face blank of any expression. "Have you reached a decision?"

"I have. Will you please give this to the ..." Rhetta stopped before she said the senator's name. "To your associate and let him know I intend to stay until Friday to begin my investigation, pending his approval and the return of a signed contract."

"I'll do that. Will you be here all evening?"

"Yes. We're going to the dining room, then we'll return to our rooms."

"Very well. Good evening, Miss Wallace." Mr. Reynolds tipped his hat and strode out the door.

Rhetta hoped her decision to find out the truth about Reed Saunders wouldn't prove to be a terrible mistake.

Chapter Three

June 1886
Holiday, Oregon

"It's a warm one today, Buddy," Rowan Reed said as he and his most faithful friend made their way into town for supplies.

The horse continued his plodding gait along the road into Holiday.

Rowan patted the animal's neck. "It sure is pretty, though, isn't it, Buddy?"

With no expectation the horse would gain the magical ability to speak and answer his questions, Rowan glanced at the tree-covered mountains around them that filled the air with a fresh scent that put him in mind of Christmas.

Not that Rowan had celebrated many special holidays in his lifetime, but the greens people used as Christmas decorations always smelled so good.

He drew in a deep breath and smiled as he rode into town. He raised a hand in greeting to R.C. Milton, owner of the blacksmith shop and livery. He and his wife had a cute little baby boy and seemed as happy as any couple could be.

Rowan had met several happy couples, all new to the union of marriage, since he'd moved to Holiday. Doctor Holt and his wife, Henley, had married last summer. Marshal Dillon Durant had married Zara Wynn, the newest schoolteacher. From what Rowan had heard, the students adored her, and talk was that more students would attend school in the fall.

Pastor John Ryan and his lively, lovely wife waved as they strode along the boardwalk in the morning sunshine. Keeva Ryan was a sister to the doctor, and nothing like what one would imagine when picturing a pastor's bride, but she and John were well suited, or so it seemed to Rowan. There was a day, a few months back, when he thought Keeva might yank every last hair from the pastor's head when he tried to play matchmaker with her and Rowan. Thankfully, Keeva had set the pastor straight on the matter. To make sure there wasn't any lingering confusion, after Keeva had stormed off, Rowan had explained to the pastor he wasn't interested in courting anyone.

His life was destined to be lived alone, and dreaming it might be something more just led to disappointment.

Rowan stopped his horse outside the post office, tied Buddy's reins to the hitching rail, and went inside to see if he had any mail. An envelope postmarked from Texas caught him by surprise. He quickly tucked it into his pocket, thanked the postmaster, and stepped outside, drawing in a lungful of air. Just the sight of the envelope made him want to race home, pack his things, and skedaddle for parts unknown.

Nevertheless, he'd decided when he'd moved to Holiday that he wouldn't leave. This place was home, and he had no interest in abandoning all his hard work in establishing his ranch. Besides, he was tired of running away from his troubles. If they came looking for him, so be it.

Rowan dragged in another lungful of air, then jumped when someone touched his arm.

He turned his head and forced a smile for Cora Lee Coleman, another of the newer brides in town. She'd married Jace, who was a train engineer. They lived at Elk Creek Ranch, the biggest, oldest, and one of the more prosperous spreads in the area, with Jace's father, Grant.

Cora Lee was a fine cook, known for miles around for the delicious meals she served. Rowan never turned down an invitation to join them for lunch because the only thing worse than paying for food at the hotel's dining room was eating his own cooking.

"Mr. Reed. It's so nice to see you," Cora Lee said, offering him a genuine smile. "How is everything at your ranch?"

"Things are good at the Double R, Mrs. Coleman. How about at Elk Creek? Did Grant get that new bull he was talking about a few weeks ago?"

Cora Lee nodded. "He did. It took Jace and four of the hands to get the beast home once they managed to unload him off the train. They've named him Herkimer. You should come to lunch Sunday after church and see him for yourself."

Rowan's smile turned from half-hearted to genuine. "Thank you for the invitation. I'd be most honored to come."

"Wonderful. We'll see you then, Mr. Reed. Enjoy this beautiful day."

"Oh, I will, Mrs. Coleman." He tipped his hat to her. "Tell Jace and Grant hello for me."

"I'll do that." She nodded to him, then headed across the street. He figured she was likely on her way to visit Henley Holt or Anne Milton. The three women were as thick as a pot of honey left in the summer sunshine.

Pleased he could look forward to a delicious meal on Sunday afternoon, Rowan crossed the street and headed into the mercantile.

"Howdy, Rowan." Rupert Rogers, owner of the mercantile, offered a friendly nod as Rowan stepped into the store.

"Hello, Rupert. How are things?"

"Good. Can't complain. Then again, it's hard to complain about anything on such a fine day, except maybe not having time to go outside and enjoy it."

"It is a fine summer day," Rowan said, glancing outside.

Rupert nodded. "What can I do for you today?"

"Just a few things," Rowan said, handing the mercantile owner his list. In another week or so, he'd drive in the wagon and place a large order, but for now, there were just a few things he needed. Well, more like wanted, but he'd suffered enough in his lifetime; he didn't think it was an extravagance to buy a little salt and sugar.

"I see you have gloves on the list," Rupert said, scanning Rowan's shopping list. "I assume you're looking for leather work gloves." At Rowan's nod, Rupert pointed behind him. "We just got a new shipment in last week. They are good quality at a very reasonable price."

"I'll take a look, Rupert. Thank you."

Rowan looked over the selection of gloves and chose two pairs. As hard as he worked on his ranch, it didn't take long for him to completely wear out a pair. The gloves he'd been wearing had holes in every finger, and the palms were falling apart. He figured it was somewhat pointless to put them on when they failed at the duty of protecting his hands.

Rupert glanced at him when two women came in. He gave the mercantile owner a tip of his head, letting him know to help the women while Rowan perused the merchandise. He thought about the invitation to lunch on Sunday and found a small box of candy to take to Cora Lee. He'd heard she liked chocolates. Aware that R.C. and Anne Milton were frequent Sunday guests at Elk Creek Ranch, Rowan wandered over to the display of books and looked for a book he could buy for their little one.

He picked up *A Child's Garden of Verses* by Robert Louis Stevenson and thumbed through the pages. The illustrations and poems appealed to him, so he decided to add it to his purchases. It wasn't like him to buy gifts or try to be friendly, but something about this community and the people in it drew him like no other place he'd ever lived.

Rowan had spent his life alone and intended to die that way, but once in a while, a little glimmer of friendship fed the empty places in his heart and gave him the strength to keep going. He was grateful to the people in Holiday who had reached out to him, made him feel welcome, even when he'd remained aloof. He figured the least he owed them were a few little tokens of gratitude.

Rowan saw a few books he might have enjoyed if he'd had the time for such leisurely pleasures, but he generally worked from before dawn until after dusk. The only reason he took time to come into town today was the fact that he'd used the last of his salt two days ago and the sugar had run out last week along with the coffee. He'd been drinking well water and making do without coffee. But salt was another matter. He couldn't abide one more tasteless egg, which was what he generally ate at least one if not two meals a day. Salt sure made the beans he cooked taste a whole heap better too.

"Find what you needed?" Rupert asked when Rowan finally made his way to the counter. He'd added two pairs of denims to his purchases since it was rare he found any in his size. At almost six-four, he was a big man with thick muscles, and finding ready-made clothes to fit often proved to be challenging.

"More than what I planned to buy today," he said as Rupert rang up his purchases. The man pointed to a jar of the candy Rowan liked. "Help yourself."

"Thanks." Rowan fished out one of the butterscotch drops and stuck it in his mouth.

After he paid the bill, Rupert wrapped his purchases into three packages. Two would go into his saddlebags, and the larger one with several items sandwiched between the two pairs of denims, would get tied on behind the saddle.

"Have an excellent day, Rowan," Rupert said as Rowan lifted the packages and headed toward the door.

"I intend to, Rupert. Enjoy your day."

Rowan had just reached for the door when it swung open. He tipped his head to Keeva Ryan as she breezed inside. "Mr. Reed. It's nice to see you in town. I hope all is well at your ranch."

"Doing very well, Mrs. Ryan. Tell the pastor I said hello."

"I will do that." She smiled at him, then turned to Rupert. "Did you get more peppermint sticks in yet?"

"I did and held a box back for you."

Rowan tried not to grin as he left and made his way back to his horse. He'd seen the pastor's wife enjoying peppermint sticks on more than one occasion. He assumed she must have a bit of a sweet tooth, or at least a strong liking for peppermint.

"Come on, Buddy," Rowan said as he swung into the saddle. "We've got a long day of work waiting for us."

That was one thing he could count on. There was always more work than Rowan could ever finish on his own, but he refused to hire anyone to help on his ranch. Not yet. Not when he could do the work of two or three men himself.

Rowan had bought a farm that a couple, Mr. and Mrs. Eggleton, had started several years ago. The wife had died in childbirth, and then the house had burned to the ground. Deep in his grief, Mr. Eggleton had sought to sell the farm and return to his relatives in the East.

Rowan had happened upon an advertisement in a newspaper for the farm and had been able to purchase the property. It included a sturdy barn and corrals, a fenced pasture, and a section of tree-covered forest at a rock-bottom price, which was all he could afford.

The first few months, he'd lived in a tent while he invested his time and effort into building more fences and then purchasing a small herd of Hereford cattle that he grazed on the expanded pastures. Once his cattle were settled, he turned his attention to cleaning up the rest of the place.

Around the perimeter of where the house had once stood, colorful flowers bloomed, adding a bit of cheer to the landscape. Rowan had labored during the evening hours clearing away the rubble from the burned house, salvaging what he could. He built a new house on a slight hill that overlooked the largest pasture. He could see for miles from that vantage point, and with the woods behind the house, it made him feel slightly protected.

He'd painted the house white and the barn red. The outhouse, chicken coop, and the three-sided shed where he parked his wagon and the few pieces of farm equipment he'd acquired he also painted red with crisp white trim.

Rowan wasn't a farmer, but he'd planted a garden, and he'd harvested enough grass hay to feed his critters through the winter last year. He hoped to cut even more to put away for the winter this year, because if they'd had just one more week of bad weather in the spring, his cattle would have gone hungry.

Maybe by next summer he'd have himself established enough to be able to consider hiring an extra hand or two.

For now, he'd make do.

After all, he had a lot of practice.

Chapter Four

"Look, Mama!" Lee pointed out the window as the train slowed, nearing their stop of Holiday, Oregon.

Rhetta refastened the pin holding her hat in place, then bent her neck slightly to better see out the window.

Lee had been almost beside himself with excitement when she'd concluded they would indeed need to travel to Oregon in their pursuit of Reed Saunders. Rhetta had enjoyed seeing the country, but she was ready to have her feet on solid ground. A bath, a hot meal, and a comfortable bed were all she wanted to think about this evening, but she had no doubt Lee would want to explore this mountain town in Eastern Oregon.

It was lovely, with the tree-covered mountains that loomed above them. When they'd traveled from Boise, Idaho, to Baker City, Oregon, Rhetta had thought the landscape stark yet magnificent with hills of rock and sagebrush and hardly a tree to be seen, other than those in the little towns they passed.

Once they departed Baker City, though, the landscape soon changed. Now, they were truly up in the mountains. The windows that let in a breeze to cool the stuffy car in the June heat also carried a refreshing, crisp scent.

"Do you think he's really here?" Lee asked as the train creaked to a stop at the Holiday depot.

Rhetta shrugged and gathered their things. "I don't know, Lee, but we'll do our best to find out. If he's here, we'll locate him. It's not like Holiday is a big city. Let's find our hotel and get settled, and tomorrow we'll rest since it is Sunday. Beginning Monday, we'll start searching."

Lee appeared slightly disappointed that she didn't desire to immediately begin searching for Reed Saunders. Her pursuit of him had taken them from Cincinnati to Chicago to Texas, up to Kansas, and back to Texas, before they'd embarked on this journey to Oregon.

Senator Tomlinson was paying for everything, but Rhetta was tired. She'd never been away from home for months at a time, and this case was wearing on her patience and nerves. The senator demanded weekly updates, which she sent in telegrams addressed to Mr. Reynolds. She didn't trust that man any more than she did the senator, but she had received the first half of her payment, part of which she'd tucked into her account at the bank, and the rest she'd hidden in the false bottom of her trunk.

When she'd requested first class accommodations for their trip to Oregon, Mr. Reynolds had balked, but he'd soon wired her money for the train tickets and their hotel stay.

At least with school out for the summer, Rhetta didn't have to try to find time to teach Lee and help with his schoolwork while working on this investigation.

Rhetta smiled and thanked the porter as he gave her a hand off the train. She moved out of the way, then took a moment just to breathe in the fresh air and get her bearings.

Lee was practically bouncing off one foot to the other in his anticipation of seeing the town. If their train hadn't been late arriving in Baker City, she would have enjoyed exploring a place that appeared to be bustling with activity. Lee had been much more interested in the ranch they'd passed and the cowhands that whooped and waved as the train rolled by the cattle they were herding.

Lee had switched from being fascinated with knights and their ladies to cowboys. When they were in Kansas, she'd purchased a pair of cowboy boots for him from a bootmaker. He'd been so elated that he'd worn them nearly every day.

The next thing he'd likely want was a gun belt like the cowboys in Kansas and Texas had worn, but that request, if it came, was where she'd draw the line. He'd likely shoot himself or her or an innocent bystander.

What Lee didn't know was that Rhetta always carried a little double shot Derringer with her. She'd taught herself to fire it with accuracy and precision, and knew, if the day ever came when she needed to defend herself, she could.

Rhetta slipped an arm around Lee's waist, no longer able to comfortably rest her arm over the top of his shoulders now that he'd neared her height. Rhetta was tall for a woman, looking most men in the eye, which was likely another reason she'd never been courted. Many of the male species felt threatened by a woman who was as tall as they.

"There! I see our trunks," Lee said, pointing to where workers unloaded the baggage car.

She took the tokens for their trunks out of her reticule. "Don't let the trunks out of your sight. I'll see about finding someone to transport them to the hotel."

Rhetta stepped into the depot office, where people milled about, and a harried-looking man stood behind the counter.

"How may I help you, ma'am?" the man asked when she stepped up to the counter.

Since he hadn't made eye contact with her, Rhetta was surprised he knew she was even there. She didn't bother to correct him that her title was miss. What did it matter anyway?

She spoke quickly, staring at the top of his head when he bent to retrieve a paper that fell to the floor. "Is there a service for hire to transport trunks to the hotel?"

"Yep. Ask for Mr. Curtis. He has a bright blue wagon. It's usually parked on the end of the platform by the baggage car."

"Thank you."

"Enjoy your stay," the man said, offering her what might have been a smile if he'd looked up from the papers he was scanning through and then stamping.

Rhetta hurried over to where Lee stood by their two trunks and looked around. She noticed a bright blue wagon with a short, heavy-set man standing in the back of it, loading trunks directly into it from the platform.

"Excuse me, sir," she said, walking over to the edge of the platform as he grabbed a steamer trunk and slid it into his wagon.

"Help you with something, ma'am?" the man asked, hefting another trunk as he looked her way.

"Are you Mr. Curtis?"

He nodded.

"Then yes. We have two trunks we'd like to have transported to the hotel. Would you be able to take them for us?"

The man nodded again and gave her the price. It was reasonable, so she pulled coins from her reticule and paid him.

"Thank you, ma'am. I'll have them over there directly. It's my second stop."

"Thank you, Mr. Curtis." Rhetta started to turn away, then looked back at him. "Where is the hotel?"

"You go straight up that street there," he said, pointing to a street that headed east from the depot.

"When you get to Main Street, you'll see the mercantile sign. Turn left and go two blocks. You can't miss the hotel."

"Thank you, sir."

The man tipped his hat to her, then Rhetta looped her arm around Lee's. "Let's go to the hotel, Lee. I'm sure by now you are on the verge of starvation, and I greatly desire the opportunity to wash away a week's worth of grime."

"I am hungry. It was sure handy that lady was selling sandwiches at the depot in Baker City. Otherwise, we wouldn't have had time to get anything to eat."

"It was providential she was there," Rhetta agreed, then crossed the street, walking away from the depot. The town was nice, small as it was, with many new buildings. She stopped when they reached Main Street, crossed the side street, and continued walking until they arrived at the hotel.

"This looks nice," Lee said as he pulled open the door and waited for her to step inside.

Rhetta walked into the lobby, shocked to discover it was comparable to any they'd stayed in during their travels. In fact, it was far nicer than the first hotel where they'd taken rooms when they'd traveled to Texas. The furniture there had been dusty and shabby, and the walls had been so thin, she could hear their neighbors snoring all night.

"Good afternoon. Welcome to the Holiday Hotel. How may we be of service to you today?" asked a friendly woman standing at the front counter. A rack full of keys hung on pegs behind her, and a vase full of fragrant flowers filled the air with a delightful scent. "I'm Mrs. Piedmont. My husband and I are the proprietors of this establishment."

"Mrs. Piedmont, it's lovely to meet you. I'm Rhetta Wallace, and this is my son, Lee. Would you have adjoining rooms, or perhaps a suite available?"

Lee beamed at her, as he did whenever she introduced him as her son. She in turn, had to swallow down her emotion every time he referred to her as his mama. It made her heart swell until she felt like it might burst.

"We're so happy to have you with us, Mrs. Wallace. I have our finest suite open. It has a sitting room with two bedrooms. Will that suffice?"

"That will do quite nicely. Thank you."

Mrs. Piedmont smiled and glanced behind Rhetta. "Do you have any baggage we may assist with?"

"Yes. Mr. Curtis will be dropping off our trunks. Is it possible to have them delivered to our room?"

"Certainly." Mrs. Piedmont jotted a note on a piece of paper. "If you'd like a nice hot bath, I can have water sent up."

Rhetta wanted nothing more, but she glanced at Lee who was hungrily eyeing the sign that pointed to the hotel's dining room.

"That would be lovely. Is your dining room open?"

"It opens in thirty minutes. If the young sir is hungry, you're welcome to enjoy the cookies we have sitting out." She pointed to a basket on a nearby table surrounded by a grouping of chairs.

"No more than three," Rhetta said, then turned back to Mrs. Piedmont. "Thank you. A bath would be much appreciated. Do we need a reservation for your restaurant?"

"Goodness, no. Just walk right in when you're ready and choose whatever table you like." The woman handed Rhetta a key with a metal disc on the end that had the room number.

"There are only two rooms on the top floor, and the other one isn't occupied. If you need anything else, please let me know."

"Thank you, Mrs. Piedmont." She motioned for Lee to join her as he stuffed the last bite of an oatmeal cookie into his mouth and carried two more with him.

"I'll have that bath water sent right up." The woman pointed toward the door. "If your son is interested in looking around town, it's perfectly safe. He might enjoy stretching his legs after traveling. I didn't even ask, but I assume you came in on today's train."

"We did, and thank you." Rhetta started up the stairs, but Lee seemed hesitant.

"May I please go for a walk, Mama? I promise not to get into trouble."

"Very well, but don't be gone too long." She took a coin from her reticule and gave it to him. "In case you get hungry before dinner, I'm sure you can find something at the mercantile."

"Thanks!" Lee kissed her cheek, then hurried outside into the bright summer day.

Rhetta turned and once again started up the stairs. Her legs grew heavier with every step until she wasn't sure she'd make it to the room at the top of the last flight of stairs, but by sheer will, she managed. After fumbling with the key to open the door, she pushed it open and drew in a gasp at the lovely suite. Decorated in soft colors with plush furnishings, it looked like a welcome haven after all the traveling she'd endured. A bedroom flanked each side of the large sitting area. A table for four occupied the space beneath the gleaming windows that allowed a broad beam of sunlight to glide into the room.

She looked in both bedrooms and then chose the one decorated in hues of pink and green for herself, leaving the yellow room for Lee.

Rhetta was in the process of removing her hat when a knock sounded at the door. She forced her weary legs back across the expansive room to open it.

"Mrs. Wallace? We have water for your bath," a smiling maid said, holding up a bucket of water. "I'm Rachel, and this is my brother, Nick, and our cousin, Rob."

"Come in, please. It's lovely to meet you," Rhetta said, motioning them inside. She watched as the maid set down the bucket, then slid back a panel in the wall and folded down a tub. "How clever!"

The maid smiled and moved back as her brother and cousin walked across the room, carrying large buckets of steaming water in their hands. They poured it into the tub, then the maid added a bucket of what Rhetta assumed was cool water. With that task complete, she stepped back into the hall but soon returned with a stack of fluffy towels and a wrapped bar of soap.

"Is there anything else we may assist with?" Rachel asked.

"No, thank you, but I so appreciate this." Rhetta hurried to give them each a coin, then closed the door and locked it. She removed her hat, gloves, and shoes, then realized she had nothing clean to wear. She'd just grabbed a shoe to put it back on to see if Mr. Curtis had arrived with their trunks when another knock sounded at the door.

She opened it to find Nick and Rob, the two men who'd carried up the buckets of water, holding her trunks.

"Oh, thank you!" she said, moving aside and directing them to place Lee's trunk in his room and her trunk in the other bedroom. She paid them for their trouble, then shut the door and locked it again.

With fresh clothing to wear, she didn't waste another moment discarding her filthy clothes and unpinning her hair. Although she would have liked to soak in the steaming water until she fell asleep, she rushed to scrub away the dirt of travel, washed her hair, then hurried into her room to dress. Rhetta's hair was still damp, but she'd changed into a light cotton dress in a pale shade of blue by the time Lee knocked on the door.

"I met two boys who work at the mercantile, Mama. They invited us to church tomorrow. May we go?"

"We certainly may." Rhetta cupped his chin and smiled at him. "I'll be in my room while you take a bath. Be sure to scrub behind your ears and between your toes and wash your hair. When you're ready, we'll go down to dinner."

"Aw, do I hafta?" Lee complained, but he was already removing his shoes.

"You hafta." Rhetta winked at him, picked up her satchel full of files, and retired to her room. There was a small table with an overstuffed chair by the window. She sank into the soft cushions, pulled out the information they'd gathered at their last stop in Texas, and began reviewing what she'd learned about the man Senator Tomlinson referred to as Reed Saunders.

It had been quite a journey, not just in miles, but in her ongoing investigative work, to arrive here in Holiday.

After the senator had agreed to her terms and wired the funds to her, Rhetta's first challenge had been to try to locate Reed's mother. She'd found the house, which had reverted to the city for unpaid taxes and been sold to a young couple. Rhetta had learned the woman who owned it had died eleven years ago and had no known relatives. Determined not to give up, Rhetta had then traveled to Texas with a sketch of what she thought Reed might look like today, along with the photographs from the senator's original file.

By showing people the photos and sketch, she had finally been able to track down Reed's employer, who'd said he never had anyone named Reed working for him but recognized the man as Silas Webster. Apparently, he'd been a good cowhand and kept to himself. After helping drive a herd of cattle to Wichita, he'd sent a note that he wasn't coming back. The rancher had forwarded the pay owed Webster to an address in a tiny town fifty miles north of Wichita that wasn't any more than a stage stop.

Rhetta knew that for a fact because she and Lee had gone there. They'd managed to find the rancher Reed had worked for there, under the name of Weston Saunders. The ranch owner there had said much the same thing as the rancher in Texas: Reed had been a hard worker, kept to himself, then suddenly announced he had to leave and would send an address later to forward his pay.

The rancher still had the Texas address he'd used to mail Reed his pay, so Rhetta and Lee had made a return trip. They had ended up staying in Fredericksburg for three weeks while she'd tracked down the last place Reed Saunders had worked.

The town had been quaint, and the hotel where they'd stayed had been surprisingly comfortable. If she'd been enjoying a holiday, Rhetta would have delighted in her time there. Lee had certainly taken to the area filled with good German food and ranchers.

To keep him busy while she worked, Rhetta had enrolled Lee in school. He'd kicked up quite a fuss about it, until he'd made friends with boys his age the first day he was there. After that, he had been most eager to attend. Lee had seemed sad when the school year had come to an end for the summer. By then, Rhetta had discovered an elderly gentleman who was a retired preacher who had once known Reed.

The preacher had informed her he couldn't and wouldn't lie about knowing Reed, but he hoped she wouldn't bring harm to a man who had already suffered greatly. She assured him all she wanted was to unearth the truth. The old preacher had informed her Reed's story wasn't his to tell, but he wished her well.

She'd kept an eye on the preacher, and when he'd gone to mail a letter, she'd followed, catching sight of the address on the envelope, addressed to Rowan Reed in Holiday, Oregon.

Now, here she was, in Holiday, searching for him, uncertain what she'd find or if he'd already moved on. The preacher didn't give her a name of an employer or an address for Reed.

However, she didn't think it would be that difficult to track him down in a small town.

The man was reportedly a hard worker. He'd fled Cincinnati with nothing. No particular skills. No money. No family, except for his mother, whom he'd left behind. He'd gone to Boston, then New York City and worked at a variety of jobs, before he'd next popped up in Virginia, where he'd worked for a blacksmith. From there, he'd turned his interests outdoors and had begun working for ranchers. He must have liked that line of work, because it was what he'd stuck with regardless of where his travels took him.

There would be time enough Monday to begin searching for Reed again. Tonight, they would eat a filling meal and go to bed early. Tomorrow, they would attend the church service. Perhaps they'd even meet some people after the service who could recommend a place for Rhetta to start looking for Reed.

She couldn't explain it, but she had the strangest feeling she'd come to the right place to finally meet the man she'd followed across the country.

Chapter Five

Rowan couldn't put his finger on it, but something had him feeling as fidgety as a roosting hen with a fox sniffing around her nest.

He'd always been a little on the jumpy side, but after reading the letter Preacher Bill Bristol had sent, Rowan's senses had been on high alert.

According to the preacher, a woman and her son had come to town searching for him. Bill couldn't remember any details about them but thought their last name was Turner. Thankfully, Bill hadn't shared any of Rowan's story with the woman or where to find him. The old man doubted she'd trek all the way to Holiday just to swap howdies with him, but Rowan wasn't so sure.

Over the years, he'd been hunted by the best private detectives money could buy. The last time he'd almost been caught had been in Texas, in a little town where Bill had spent several years preaching. He'd taken Rowan under his wing, and they'd shared many a cup of awful coffee around Bill's table before Rowan's past had eventually caught up to him and he'd once again had to run.

Although he appreciated the note from Bill, Rowan's stomach tightened, hating the thought of someone else looking for him. However, the fact that the one doing the searching was a woman and her son made him think maybe this had nothing to do with the reason he'd spent the last dozen years moving from place to place, never bothering to set down roots or even fully unpack his bag.

Preacher Bill had included a written prayer in his note. Rowan thought about it as he fed and watered his animals. Perhaps he should take the old man's advice, turn all his worries over to God, and trust that everything would turn out the way it should. He knew worrying wasn't any more useful than a rocking chair caught in the wind. It created a whole lot of motion, but it didn't accomplish a single thing.

A heart-weary sigh rolled out of Rowan as he removed his socks and boots—he hadn't bothered with a shirt—and left them on the porch. He grabbed a towel and bar of soap he'd set out earlier, whistled for his dogs, Kitty and Buck, and strolled down to the creek.

The dogs chased each other and played while he took a bath. The water was cool and felt good after the exertion of seeing to his morning chores. He scrubbed his skin and hair, dove under a few times to rinse off the soap, then strode to the bank and out of the water, toweling himself dry. With the towel wrapped around his waist, he gathered the soap, his dirty pants, and drawers, whistled to the dogs again, and returned to the house, where he dressed in one of the new pairs of denims he'd purchased earlier in the week, his best shirt, and a lightweight vest. He likely should have wrangled on a tie for the church service, but he couldn't bear the thought of one strangling him on a hot day like today.

Although his clothing was informal for church, unless someone was getting married or buried, Rowan had no intention of donning the one suit he owned. Especially not on a day that was already hot enough to make him break out in a sweat just sitting in the shade.

He hoped the chocolates he'd purchased for Cora Lee Coleman wouldn't melt into an oozing mess before he could deliver them to her at lunch.

Rowan packed a few things in his saddlebags, settled a hat on his head, and went out to saddle Buddy. He arrived to a quiet churchyard, as he generally did. He liked to be the last one in the door, take a seat in the back pew, and leave before anyone could engage him in idle talk about the weather or ask pointed questions about his past.

He made his way up the steps and through the open door of the church, then slid onto the aisle seat in the last pew.

Pastor Ryan nodded his head once to Rowan in greeting, then chose a familiar hymn for them to sing.

All through the service, Rowan felt as though eyes were watching him, but that was impossible since no one was behind him and the only other people on the pew with him were the widow Busby, and Mr. Wagner, an old man everyone called Gramps. If Rowan wasn't mistaken there was romance brewing between the older couple. He might have laughed at the notion, but who was he to judge? As far as he was concerned, love didn't have an expiration date, but what did he know about relationships and romance?

Nothing.

Or too much.

Perhaps it depended on the perspective.

Rowan forced his thoughts back to the service and listened as the pastor talked about faith. His words struck a chord with Rowan, especially when he'd just been lecturing himself about not worrying earlier. Faith meant letting go of fear. That's exactly what he needed to do. Release his fears and learn to live without constantly looking over his shoulder.

He bowed his head and sent up a prayer for help and guidance, then joined the congregation in singing the final hymn.

Rowan waited to stand until the pastor and his vibrant wife had passed by him, then he quickly moved to the door. John and Keeva Ryan were waiting there to shake hands with the members of the congregation in attendance that morning.

"We're glad to have you with us today, Rowan," John said, with a pleased smile. "How are things at the ranch?"

"Coming along. I built another section of fence this week."

"That's grand. Will you bring in more cattle soon?"

Rowan caught sight of a woman he didn't recognize speaking to Henley Holt. He shifted slightly, so his back was to her. "I'll wait until spring, but at least the pastures will be ready."

"That they will."

Rowan nodded politely to Keeva, then hustled down the steps and out to the hitching rail, where he'd left Buddy tied with other horses.

Without waiting to get caught in idle conversation, he rode away from the church, heading east out of town, then taking a deer trail through the woods that would put him back on the road out to Elk Creek Ranch. Just in case anyone had been watching him from the church, he didn't want them to know his destination.

Generally, Jace and Cora Lee Coleman didn't mention their invited guests to others, so he felt confident that, other than them, and perhaps the Milton family, no one else was privy to his plans to join them for lunch.

He waited at the end of their lane for their buggy to arrive. Jace waved, and Cora Lee smiled as they passed by him and continued on toward the house. Rowan followed them and dismounted at the barn. He removed Buddy's saddle, knowing from past visits that Jace would have him turn the horse loose in the pasture by the barn. He'd just pulled the gifts from his saddlebag when Jace stopped the buggy outside the barn and got out.

After greeting him with handshakes, Jace grinned at him. "Glad you could join us today, Rowan. It's sure a warm day for June, isn't it?"

"It is warm," Rowan agreed as he helped Jace unhitch the horse from the buggy. It wasn't long until R.C. arrived. Once the horses were taken care of, the three men walked back to the house.

A cloth fluttered on the table set up beneath the trees, where there was shade and a cooling breeze.

"This is nice," Rowan said, moving into the shade out of the hot sun.

"It is," R.C. agreed, heading toward the front door. "I'll set this inside for Anne."

"Actually, I have something for the baby," Rowan said, feeling embarrassed as he held out the book.

R.C. grinned and whacked him on the shoulder. "Come give it to Anne. She'll be so pleased."

Rowan glanced at Jace, then followed R.C. into the large living room. The heat from the kitchen had filled the house, even though Cora Lee had all the windows open to let the breeze blow through. The screen door slapped shut behind Rowan, and he wanted to nervously fidget after he removed his hat.

Anne was just handing Charles to Grant Coleman, while he sat in a rocking chair by a rock fireplace that was cozy and comforting in the winter.

"Howdy, Rowan. Glad you could join us," Grant said, motioning him to move farther inside. "Hot enough for you, son?"

"Yes, sir. I believe it is," Rowan said with a grin. He liked the Coleman family, and R.C. and

Anne as well. They were good people who never asked too many questions, and they made him feel welcome.

"Rowan has something for Charles," R.C. said, giving Anne a little nudge forward.

"It's just a book I saw at the mercantile. I know he's too little for it now, but he might enjoy it later." Rowan held out the book.

Anne took it from him, and her eyes glistened with unshed tears. "That is so very kind of you, Mr. Reed. Thank you for thinking of our son." She opened the book and glanced at the first poem and illustration. "Oh, it's lovely! We'll read him a poem every night before his bedtime. He'll love looking at the illustrations. Thank you so much, Mr. Reed."

"It's Rowan, and you're welcome." He gave the woman one of his rare, genuine smiles, then took a step toward the kitchen. "I brought some chocolates for you, Mrs. Coleman, but I'm not sure what the heat did to them."

"Candy? For me?" Cora Lee asked, then wiped her hands on her apron and hurried over to take the box from him. "What a wonderful treat, Mr. Reed. Thank you."

"Call me Rowan, and you're welcome. I didn't think about it being so hot when I bought them."

"That's perfectly fine. Jace, will you put them in the springhouse? It will chill them. If nothing else, we can spoon the candy over the ice cream we'll enjoy later."

Jace took the candy and went out the back door.

Rowan perked up at the mention of ice cream. He loved it even though he didn't get to enjoy it often. "Yes, ma'am. That sounds delicious."

Cora Lee smiled and handed Rowan and R.C. each a bowl. "Take those out to the table, please. We'll be ready to eat in just a few minutes."

Fifteen minutes later, Grant asked a blessing on the meal they'd all gathered around, then food and conversation flowed. Cora Lee and Anne discussed the new woman and her son who had been at church that morning. From the information they'd gathered, the woman's name was Rhetta Wallace, and the boy's name was Lee.

Finding out the woman's name set Rowan's mind at ease since Preacher Bill had said the woman looking for him was named Turner. For the first time that day, Rowan relaxed and let his tense shoulders slide back down to their normal position. He helped himself to a second roll and slathered it with Cora Lee's delicious berry jam.

"She didn't say why she was in town, but she seemed nice," Cora Lee said as she passed a bowl of creamed peas and potatoes to Rowan, still discussing the mystery woman.

From the glimpse he'd had of the visitor at church, she also seemed quite pretty with an abundance of brown hair and a tall, curvaceous figure. She likely had a husband she'd come to meet. Perhaps he was a miner in the area, but she seemed dressed too elegantly, her clothes too expensive, for that to be the case. Maybe her man had bought some land or was planning to open a business in town.

Regardless of her reason for being in Holiday, Rowan knew he was wasting his time to give her a second thought.

As though he sensed Rowan's desire to change the subject, Jace glanced from him to R.C. "Did you read in the newspaper about Grover Cleveland's wedding? It seems he is the first president to be married while in office, and at the White House."

"I saw that article," Anne said, then gave Cora Lee a dreamy smile. "Miss Frances Folsom is only twenty-one, and the youngest First Lady. From the article, it sounded like they had a lovely ceremony. Everyone knows she's always in the height of fashion."

Jace and R.C. exchanged looks that said they had no care for talk of fashion.

"What do you think of the expanding cattle industry in Montana? There was an article in the paper about that the other day." Jace looked to Rowan.

He might not know anything about fashion or news that made the social pages, but he knew cattle. He and the men discussed cattle breeds, ranching techniques, and horses as the ladies discussed dignitaries, weddings, and a trip to Baker City to their favorite dress shop.

After they'd all eaten until they were stuffed, the men did the dishes while Anne and Cora Lee checked on little Charles, who had been asleep in the shade.

"Come take a look at Herkimer," Grant said when the last dish had been dried and put away.

"He's a dandy," R.C. said, following behind Rowan as Jace led the way outside. Cora Lee and Anne glanced up at them from the blanket they'd spread on the grass, saw where they were headed, and returned to talking about the improvement committee they were working to establish in town.

Rowan admired the two women. They were kind, sweet, generous, and caring. They were both pretty in different ways. Anne spoke with a British accent, and the best word he could think of to describe her was impeccable. Her match with the burly blacksmith seemed improbable, but it was clear Anne and R.C. were deeply in love. The word that came to mind when he thought of Cora Lee was capable. He had no doubt Jace had chosen well in marrying her. She was the type of woman to stand steadfast and true through the storms of life as well as the triumphs and joys.

If Rowan ever lost every last speck of sense and decided to get married, he wanted a wife like Cora Lee. One that would not just stand beside him but walk with him through whatever came their way.

Since he was certain he'd never have all his brains roll out his ears, he knew he'd remain single the remainder of his days.

However, the long, lonely future stretching out before him didn't seem as awful as it used to now that he'd made a few friends.

That's surely what he'd call Jace and R.C., even Pastor John Ryan and the marshal. Rowan had tried avoiding the lawman, but Marshal Dillon

Durant had been just as welcoming and friendly as everyone else in Holiday.

Rowan knew if he ever needed someone to watch his back, they would without asking any questions or giving a moment of hesitation. If any of them needed it, he'd do the same for them.

When they reached the pasture, Rowan leaned his arms on the top rail of a pole fence. "Now that is a bull," he said as he admired Grant's heavy-chested Angus bull. Grant looked like a proud papa as he pointed out the bull's finer points.

After giving the new bovine several moments of attention, Jace asked R.C. to take a look at one of the horses that had been acting off, so they ventured into the barn where Jace had moved the horse into a stall. Rowan agreed with R.C.'s diagnosis and suggested treatment.

He'd been in town long enough to learn R.C. was the closest thing they had to a veterinarian, unless someone could talk Doctor Holt into treating their animals, which Gramps had been known to do on occasion.

Rowan had heard Henley describing the day the old man had tried to bring his burro into the office. Evan had threatened to shoot them both, then promptly gone out and treated the animal.

The doctor was another of the good people Rowan had met. He and his wife worked long hours, often without adequate compensation, and never complained. He hoped the town realized how fortunate they were to have a doctor as skilled as Evan in their midst.

"Let's get that ice cream churning," Jace finally said, rubbing his hands together in anticipation as they walked back to the house.

Cora Lee had already started turning the handle that moved the paddle inside the jar of ice cream, so Grant took over.

"Sing for us," R.C. prompted, giving his wife a warm look.

Anne glanced at Jace. He nodded and began singing "What a Friend We Have in Jesus."

Rowan took a turn at the crank on the ice cream churn, listening to songs Jace and Anne sang with an appreciative ear.

On a beautiful summer day, about to enjoy ice cream and cake, surrounded by friends, Rowan didn't know when he'd ever felt as content.

Chapter Six

Rowan removed his hat, wiped sweat onto a handkerchief he pulled from the pocket of his filthy denims, then took a long swig of water from the canteen he'd brought out to where he was cutting grass with a scythe and then raking it into rows. Once it dried, he would pack it into the barn loft. Eventually, he planned to build a shed to store it, away from the other buildings in case the hay ever sparked and started to burn. For now, though, he figured the barn would have to do.

The sun was high overhead although not quite as relentlessly hot as it had been the past week.

Still, he hadn't bothered to put on a shirt, knowing he'd discard it as soon as he got to work. Besides, no one else was there to see him, unless Buddy and the dogs counted, and they wouldn't have cared if he'd paraded around naked as the day he was born.

Amused by thoughts of how uncomfortable it would be to work without his clothes on, Rowan settled the hat back on his head, tucked the soggy handkerchief into his pocket and picked up the scythe again.

He'd only cut a few feet when dust coming up the lane alerted him to a visitor. He glanced down at his bare chest. It was too far to the house to get his shirt, even if he'd been inclined to go, which he wasn't.

Rarely did anyone venture out to the Double R Ranch, and that's how Rowan liked it. He leaned on the scythe and waved as Pastor Ryan rode past the house and barn and out to where Rowan worked.

"Morning, John. What brings you all the way out here?"

The pastor swung off his horse, left him ground-tied, and walked over to Rowan, careful not to disturb the neat rows he'd already raked together.

"You're pretty handy at farming for being a rancher," John said, looking around at the grass Rowan had cut already that morning.

"It's a necessary evil. I hope in a few more years I'll be able to buy equipment for mowing and a hay fork."

"They've got new inventions coming out faster than I can keep track of them," John said, not seeming the least bit disturbed by Rowan's appearance. "I didn't come out to keep you from your work. In fact, if I didn't have another matter to which I need to attend, I'd offer to stay and help."

Rowan remembered then that the pastor had grown up on a farm. There were likely things he knew far more about than Rowan did when it came to farm work. “I might take you up on that another day.”

“Let’s plan on it. It would feel good to get out and swing a scythe, at least for a little while.” The pastor sighed and took another step closer to Rowan. “I don’t know if you happened to notice we had two new faces at church on Sunday. Rhetta Wallace and her son, Lee. She’s been asking around town in regard to a man named Reed Saunders. I have no idea why she’s seeking Reed Saunders, and I don’t need to, although the person she’s describing sounds like you. That said, if you ever need to talk, Rowan, my door is always open, and anything you share will be kept in confidence.”

“Thank you, John, for the offer, and letting me know about the woman. I can honestly say I have no idea who she is or what she wants. I was planning to come into town tomorrow for supplies anyway. If she’s still around, I’ll stop by and speak with her. Is she staying at the hotel?”

John nodded and started back to his horse. “She is. I didn’t get the idea she’s planning on leaving Holiday anytime soon. She’s having tea right now with Keeva.”

“I see,” Rowan said, but he didn’t. Why was some woman he’d never heard of looking for him, and why did she have her son with her? Rowan knew for a fact he’d not fathered any children, so if she tried to claim the boy was his, she’d be wrong. He might have concluded a nightmare from his past was breathing down his neck, but it wouldn’t involve an elegantly dressed woman and her boy.

"Don't ever be afraid to knock on my door, Rowan. Anytime. Day or night." John held out a hand, and Rowan shook it.

"Thank you, John. Thanks for being a friend as well as a mighty fine pastor."

John's chest swelled slightly, then he removed his hat. "Mind if I say a little prayer before I leave?"

"Not at all." Rowan removed his hat, bowed his head, and listened as the pastor offered a prayer for Rowan's keeping and for him to have strength and wisdom in whatever tomorrow might bring.

"Thanks again, John. I appreciate your making the trip out here."

"Of course, Rowan. I'll see you Sunday at church if not before."

"I'll be there."

Rowan waved after John mounted and started back toward the road. As he worked, he thought about what John had said. It was nice to know he could talk to the pastor anytime if he felt the need.

His mind played over why the woman was looking for him, though. Could she possibly be the one Preacher Bill had mentioned? But he'd said the woman's name was Turner. Or maybe she'd lied about her name to Preacher Bill, and to the people of Holiday. For all he knew, her name could be Gertrude Gobozelwitz.

Entertained by the fictional name, he leaned on the scythe and looked around at the plentiful rows of cut grass. If nothing else, his anxiety was good for getting a wealth of work finished.

After a lunch of fried eggs and ham with a glass of cool well water, he settled in the shade beneath the cottonwood tree by the house and took a nap. He was tired, and his body needed the rest before he headed back out for an afternoon of hard labor.

The sound of a buggy's jingling harness awakened him. He glanced at the sun and saw it had been at least an hour since he'd stretched out, intending to take just a ten-minute nap.

Rowan hopped up and marched over to the well. Quickly drawing a bucket full of water, he dumped it over his head, hoping to wash away dirt and sweat before whoever was approaching arrived. He gave his head a shake to dislodge the water droplets clinging to it, and then ran a hand down his chest to sluice away what he could as a buggy stopped in front of the house.

He strode around the house and came to a halt at the sight of the woman he'd seen at church stepping out of the buggy. She wore another expensive gown, this one pale blue, with a straw hat perched at a sassy angle on her crown of lustrous brown hair.

She smiled as she headed toward him, her stride purposeful, and her expression filled with determination.

It wasn't until she stopped a few feet away that Rowan realized her eyes were the prettiest shade of blue he'd ever seen. In fact, the woman was a beauty, with her cute, upturned nose and delectably full lips. She was even taller than he'd thought, with a figure full of curves.

Her gaze fastened on him as she pretended not to notice his bare chest or the fact that he smelled worse than one of Mr. Wagner's goats.

"Mr. Reed. Rowan Reed?" she asked, tilting her head slightly as though she was memorizing every detail of his face.

"That's right. I'm Rowan. You must be Mrs. Wallace. I heard you and your son were visiting Holiday. Is your husband working in the area?"

She shook her head. "I'm not married, Mr. Reed. I never have been. It's just easier to let people assume I am a missus than explain all the details. You see, Lee is my adopted son although he's not legally adopted because we could never actually trace his birth records. His name is Leland Turner."

The name Turner landed like a load of bricks tumbling off a wagon into Rowan's stomach. Preacher Bill hadn't been entirely wrong about the name of the woman pestering him with questions about Rowan.

Rather than show his dismay, he did his best to look friendly. "What brings you to Holiday, Miss Wallace?"

"You," she said, holding his gaze, as though she dared him to turn tail and run, which was exactly what he felt like doing.

Instead of giving in to the urge, he rocked back on one hip, doing his best to appear at ease and relaxed despite the ringing in his ears and the feeling that a freight train was bearing down on him with no hope of his escaping the oncoming collision. "Why me?"

"May we sit in the shade, sir? It may take more than a minute to explain." Rhetta glanced behind him toward the shade trees.

Rowan motioned to the porch, where he'd built a bench out of split logs. It wasn't fancy, but it provided a place to sit in the evenings, which he didn't get to do very often. However, the dogs enjoyed the seat and often took their naps there.

He pulled the soggy handkerchief from his pocket and brushed at one end of the bench, dislodging dog hair, a few burrs, and the remnants of a gnawed-on bone Kitty had been chewing the past few days.

To her credit, Miss Wallace didn't so much as grimace as she settled onto the seat, then gave him an expectant look.

Barely holding back a sigh, Rowan took a seat on the other end of the bench. "Now, why are you looking for me? I don't know you or your son, and there is no possibility I'm his father."

She smirked, actually smirked at him. "I'm aware of that, Mr. Reed. The purpose of my visit has nothing to do with Lee and everything to do with your brother."

"I don't have a brother." Rowan spoke the truth. He was his mother's only child.

"Hmm." The noise she made in her throat as she opened the file she was holding irritated him. When she extracted a photograph Rowan had hoped to never see again and held it out to him, he battled the urge to crumple it into a ball. In the image, he stood with his childhood best friend, both so happy and carefree before life had changed in a blink.

"This boy," she tapped her finger on Ricky's face, "is the son of Senator Richard Tomlinson. The second boy," she tapped Rowan's image, "is Reed Saunders. I believe he is also a son to the senator although the man refuses to confirm that vital detail."

Rowan shook his head. "My name is Rowan Reed. I'm sorry you've come from wherever you were all the way to Holiday on a fool's errand."

The woman didn't seem bothered in the least by his words as she took out another photograph. It was of the senator with his wife and Ricky. Rowan had never seen it, at least that he could recall, but there was no denying the resemblance between the senator and Ricky, as well as Rowan.

Although he hated it, he could see the senator's face every time he looked into a mirror.

Rowan and Ricky had been friends before they realized how much they resembled each other. It had taken several months before Rowan had worked up the courage to ask his mother if Richard Tomlinson was his father. She had vehemently denied it, but Rowan had known it was true. Known it the first time he'd gone to Ricky's house to play after school and the senator had mistaken him for Ricky, then looked at him with such horror, he'd choked on his drink and hastily left the room.

The senator had tried to keep Ricky from associating with him. The man had transferred Ricky to a boarding school, but it had done no good. Ricky had run away four times, coming to find Rowan, before the senator had finally concluded the two boys would be friends no matter what he did.

Ricky had returned to the school Rowan was attending, and they'd remained friends until the day Ricky had died.

A day Rowan wanted to forget had ever happened.

Yet, here was this fancy woman flapping the tragic memories of his past in his face like the unfurling of a silk fan in a ballroom while asking questions that were none of her business.

He decided to ask a few questions of his own. "Where are you from, Miss Wallace?"

"Chicago. I grew up there."

"Family there?" Maybe she'd forget about pestering him if he distracted her.

She shook her head, and he noticed sadness in her expression. "No. No family. They're gone."

"Gone? Passed?"

A nod. He glanced at her and saw tears welling in those beautiful peepers. Not tears. He could handle rattlesnakes, rustlers, tornadoes, and wildfires, but not a woman's tears.

"I'm sorry, Miss Wallace. Were you close to them?"

She sniffled—a dainty sound that tugged at a tiny corner of his heart that hadn't yet turned to stone—and nodded again. "I had just one sister. I was two when Doni was born, and I adored her. We were the grandest of playmates. When she was four, we were playing outside in the yard with our dolls. I went inside to get a drink of water, and when I came out, she was gone. We searched everywhere. The police launched an investigation. My father was a Pinkerton detective, and it was thought she was taken by someone tied to one of his cases. She was never found. Not even so much as her hair ribbon. It broke my mother's heart. She died a few years later. My father was murdered when I was seventeen. It was then I found my purpose in life and haven't looked back once I began down this path."

"Path?" Rowan felt like he'd rammed his head into a bin full of grain, the kernels plugging his ears and clogging his thoughts. Confused and agitated, he frowned at the woman. "What path are you talking about, Miss Wallace?"

"I'm a private detective, Mr. Reed. I have been since I was seventeen. I used to help my father with his case notes, and I was good at piecing together information. My first case was finding his murderer, which I successfully completed. I went into business for myself and have been a detective for almost twelve years."

"Twelve years? Well, you certainly …" He snapped his mouth shut before he said something he shouldn't about her age. Instead, he waded through the information she'd shared since arriving uninvited on his land. "The senator you mentioned. He hired you to find this Reed Saunders person, is that correct?"

"Yes. It might have taken less time and been far easier if the senator had been forthcoming with all the facts, but since he hasn't been, it has made for certain … challenges. Mr. Saunder's mother has passed, so I couldn't ask questions of her. The man who was sheriff at the time of Ricky's death has seemed to have disappeared. I was unable to locate him to inquire about his recollections of the shooting of Ricky Tomlinson. The senator has been searching for Reed Saunders for a dozen years and has come close to catching him several times. We traveled to Texas, then to Kansas, and ended up back in Texas, following where the trail led us. It took a few weeks of searching, but I finally encountered an old preacher who recalled a young man fitting Reed's description. He was an honest man, but also evasive when it came to answering my questions. After our conversation ended, I waited around the corner from his house and followed him. He went directly to the post office, and I managed to get a look at the letter, addressed to Rowan Reed in Holiday, Oregon."

She sat back looking pleased with herself. Far too pleased for Rowan's liking.

"I do know Preacher Bill and have for years. He helped me through a dark time of my life and because of him I opened my heart to Jesus. That doesn't mean I'm the man you're searching for, Miss Wallace. Preacher Bill corresponds with me on a fairly regular basis."

She tilted her head, seemed to consider his comments, and then gave him a look full of daring. "Are you Reed Saunders?" she asked. "Did you kill Ricky?"

"Regardless of what you've been told, or think you know, I've never killed anyone. It's time for you to go, Miss Wallace. Go back to Chicago, or wherever it is you came from, and tell the senator there is no Reed Saunders living in Holiday."

Gracefully, Rhetta gathered her things, tucking the photographs back in the file. As she did, Rowan stood and couldn't help but admire the slender column of her neck, the wispy tendrils of hair framing her face, or how her name seemed so well chosen for such a magnificent looking woman.

Rhetta turned and stared at him for a full minute, which felt like half of eternity, before she moved toward the steps. "I'm staying at the Holiday Hotel if you wish to speak with me."

"I can guarantee, lady, I have no desire to speak with you more than I already have."

Liar! The voice in his head condemned him. Rowan wanted to speak with her, just to hear her sultry voice, but he certainly had no interest in discussing the subject of Ricky or his father.

"Good day, Mr. Reed." She gave him a dismissive glare, then started down the steps just as Kitty and Buck raced up them, bumping into her. The animals weren't any more used to company than Rowan was. They didn't know how to behave around a woman, especially one with her skirts twisting into a trap around her legs.

Miss Wallace lost her balance, dropped her file, and began to fall. Before she could land on her nose, Rowan jumped over the porch railing and caught her against his chest.

"Down, you two!" he hollered at the dogs who were still jumping around, tails wagging in excitement. "Stay down!"

The dogs retreated to their bench, while Rowan glanced down at the top of Miss Wallace's head. Her hat had shifted, so it perched on one side, and her hair threatened to tumble loose from the pins confining it.

The delicate fragrance of flowers floated up from her to tantalize his nose while the soft feel of her pressed against him ignited a whole different kind of heat than the summer sun pouring down on him.

She sucked in a startled gasp. He moved his hands from her arms to span her waist, setting her upright at the base of the steps beside him. He didn't release his hold on her, though. In fact, it felt as though his fingers had welded themselves to the fine fabric of her gown.

Her gloved hands slid up his chest, seemingly of their own volition, while her spectacular blue eyes widened and deepened in color. Her lips parted, ever so slightly, and Rowan found himself dipping his head, intent on tasting them.

Suddenly, she wrenched away from him, and he felt a chill sweep over his body, as though something vital had been ripped away.

"I … You …" Rhetta's chest heaved as she glowered at him.

Like any man with blood pumping through his veins, he couldn't help but notice the rise and fall of it.

She took another step back. "You're incorrigible!"

"Probably," he said, unable to hide a smirk while she appeared flustered and infuriated. Before she felt the need to slap his face, he bent down to retrieve her file.

While she situated her hat and adjusted her skirts, he picked up her papers, returning them to the file. When she wasn't looking, he took the photograph of him with Ricky, stuffing it into his pocket, then stood and held the file out to her.

"Maybe if you didn't have your nose turned high enough to drown in a rainstorm, you wouldn't face the danger of falling down the steps."

She snatched the file from his hand with a huff. "If you and your ruffian dogs had more manners than swine, I wouldn't have been in danger in the first place. Good day to you, sir!"

He watched the alluring swish of her skirts as she marched out to the buggy, climbed onto the seat, snapped the lines, and turned around in a great cloud of dust.

Rowan returned to the porch and took a seat on the bench between the two dogs. He rubbed their backs and grinned at them. "Good dogs. You are good, good dogs."

If Miss Rhetta Wallace darkened his doorstep a second time, he'd be sure to have the dogs nearby. With any luck, they'd knock her into his arms again.

Chapter Seven

"The way to a man's heart is through his stomach," Rhetta mumbled to her image in the mirror as she adjusted a wispy curl by her ear.

"What was that, Mama?" Lee asked as he walked into the room from his bedroom.

"Nothing, darling boy. Shall we proceed with our plans for the day?"

Lee nodded as he bit into a biscuit, one of a handful he'd saved from breakfast. In the two weeks they'd been in Holiday, she'd had to purchase him a new pair of pants and two new shirts. He'd simply outgrown his clothes.

He'd begged her for a pair of denims like all the cowboys and a good portion of the men in town seemed to wear. She'd agreed, buying them slightly big in hopes he'd be able to wear them longer than a month before they were too short for him.

Between his growth spurts and nonstop eating, Lee had spent their time in town making friends with the two boys who worked at the mercantile. When they'd finished up their work yesterday, the three of them had gone fishing, a new experience for Lee, and one he wouldn't likely forget. He'd been so proud of the fish he caught, showing them off to Rhetta before giving them to his friend Benji to take home to his mother to fry for their supper.

Rhetta had never seen Lee look so happy and carefree, so much like a child, as he had since they'd arrived in Holiday. She was in no rush to return to Chicago or to deal with Senator Tomlinson. She was as certain as the sun would set that evening that Rowan Reed was the senator's son. He looked so much like the senator, the resemblance would have been uncanny, had she not already concluded they were related. Yet, Rowan had clearly and emphatically refused to answer her questions about being Reed Saunders.

She'd considered the conversation many times since she'd gone out to his ranch. He hadn't outright denied being Reed, but he hadn't confessed to it either. He had seemed quite genuine, though, when he adamantly stated he hadn't killed anyone.

Rhetta believed him. All along, she'd felt there was more to Ricky's story than what the senator had shared, but until Rowan Reed was ready to speak to her about what had happened that day, she'd never know the truth.

And the truth was what she sought, regardless of what the senator wanted.

Until she had it, she refused to disclose any details about Rowan to the senator. The weekly report she sent to Mr. Reynolds only conveyed she was still searching for a positive identity of Reed Saunders. She might be positive she'd found him, but Senator Tomlinson and his cronies didn't need to be made aware of the fact.

Rhetta's thoughts wandered to the afternoon she'd visited the Double R Ranch, as Rowan had dubbed his property. It was bad enough the man didn't possess the common decency to put on a shirt and had sat bare chested the whole time they'd talked, but then she'd tripped over his dogs on the steps. When he'd pulled her against him to keep her from falling on her face, she'd never experienced such warmth. She felt not only surrounded by it but engulfed in the heat of him. In his masculine scent. In the acres of golden skin on display and the hard rigid contours of his muscled physique.

Through her work, Rhetta had seen things most ladies would not, so it wasn't her first exposure to a man's bare chest, but none she'd seen had looked as … impressive as Rowan Reed's. Hard physical labor had honed every muscle of his body.

As they'd spoken on that filthy, crude bench of his, she'd done her best to keep her eyes on his handsome face, which wasn't exactly a hardship. However, when he'd glanced away or was looking at the photographs she'd handed to him, she'd let her gaze graze over his form, noting scars that had healed but must have been painful when he'd sustained them. His arms appeared powerful enough to rip a person in half, if he were so inclined.

He wouldn't though.

Despite his brawny build and towering height, she sensed a gentleness in him he tried to hide behind his gruff demeanor.

Rimmed with dark lashes, his eyes were gray and stormy. She'd seen them fill with sadness and regret when she mentioned Ricky, mirth when she'd called him incorrigible, and something she had yet to identify when he'd been holding her close to him with his hands bracketing her waist. He'd lifted her with such ease, it was as though she weighed nothing, which she knew wasn't true.

For a brief moment, she'd wished she hadn't been wearing her gloves so she could have felt the texture of his skin. She hadn't even been aware of her hands gliding over his chest muscles until his head had bent toward hers, his gaze locked on her mouth, as though he'd intended to kiss her.

Not once in her life had she allowed a man to kiss her, and Rhetta had no intention of her first kiss being from a man who couldn't or wouldn't tell her the truth about himself and his past. She wanted her first kiss to come from a man who loved her so deeply and completely, he would do anything to be with her.

She was certain a man like that didn't exist. One who could accept her career. One who would welcome Lee and love him as his own son. One who wouldn't bark orders and expect her to be a domestic slave. No, she wanted a man who saw her as a true partner.

Which was why she was resolved to remaining single. No man would ever see her as an equal, treat her the way she wished to be treated, or love her the way she longed to be loved.

Besides, she had more important things to focus on than pining after something that would never be.

She needed to dig the truth out of Rowan Reed whether he wanted her to or not.

Based on Lee's constant interest in food and the hungry appetites of most men she'd ever encountered, she was sure the way to get her foot into the proverbial door with Rowan was through his stomach.

"Let's go, darling boy." Rhetta gave her image one last glance, picked up her reticule, handed Lee his hat, and then opened the door to their suite.

"Tell me again what we're doing?" Lee asked as he followed her out into the hallway and closed the door.

"We're going to visit Mr. Reed at his ranch today. I thought it might be nice to take lunch out to him."

"And you think he's the man we're looking for?"

Rhetta nodded. She'd never kept anything from Lee and wouldn't begin now. "I do, but I don't wish to impart that knowledge to the senator or his men until we have proof beyond any imaginable doubt."

Lee nodded. "I don't trust or like the lot of them."

Rhetta leaned closer to him as they walked down the stairs. "I don't either, which is why we'll keep Mr. Reed's identity between us."

When they reached the lobby, they stopped at the front counter. Edith Piedmont smiled at them. "It's a beautiful day for a picnic. The chef should have your basket ready. I'll go fetch it for you."

"Thank you so much, Edith." Rhetta offered the woman who had become a friend the past two weeks a warm smile.

Lee wasn't the only one who had enjoyed life in the small town of Holiday. It was such a refreshing change from the bustle, noise, smells, and danger of Chicago. Here, Lee could wander around with his friends with no fear of being shot at by a drunk, run over by a careless wagon driver, or kidnapped.

Rhetta didn't feel the need to constantly be on guard, for both her and Lee. The residents of the town were friendly, and the community as a whole cared for one another.

There were saloons in town, and even a bawdy house called the Ruby Palace, but they were on the outskirts. From what Rhetta had observed, there were unspoken boundaries the inhabitants of those places didn't cross if they didn't want Marshal Durant to haul them to jail.

In the time she'd been in town, Rhetta had become friends with the marshal's wife as well as the pastor's new bride. The two women were so different, but both were full of knowledge and fun.

They'd all gone to an afternoon tea earlier in the week, hosted by Anne Milton. Anne, who came to America from England, had served the best cup of tea Rhetta had ever tasted. Keeva had brought berry tarts that were divine, but it was the friendship and kindness shown by the women that Rhetta had most enjoyed.

An afternoon spent with women she admired, sipping tea and savoring their company, was a novelty for Rhetta. She rarely had time for such things back home, even if she'd had any friends to spend time with, which she didn't. The closest she had to friends were her cousins and their spouses, but it wasn't the same.

Here, she'd already found true friends. People she would greatly miss when the time came for her and Lee to return to Chicago.

With the way Lee had blossomed here in Holiday, she hated to think about forcing him to leave, but she couldn't very well live here. The things she hated most about a big city were what kept her employed. Liars. Thieves. Philanderers. Murderers. She was paid, and paid well, to ferret them out.

The closest thing to a crime she'd witnessed since arriving in Holiday had been two drunks singing at the top of their lungs last Saturday evening as they'd ridden out of town.

Rhetta concluded she'd become jaded in the years since her father had been killed and she'd started working as a private detective. She assumed the worst about people until they proved otherwise, and that was a terrible way to walk through life. She recognized the fact, but what could she do about it? Nothing, if she intended to return to Chicago and continue in her current line of work.

Investigating situations and people was all she'd ever done. What else could she possibly do to earn money? She was good at organization. Keeping files. Processing vast quantities of information and distilling pertinent details. Writing reports and letters. Still, there wasn't any work in Holiday to which she was suited.

Regardless of how much she and Lee liked the town, once the matter with Reed Saunders was settled, they would return to Chicago.

Today, though, was a beautiful summer day, and even if they shared their lunch with the grumpy rancher she'd found to be both attractive and annoying, she intended to enjoy the day.

"Here you are!" Edith set a large picnic basket on the counter, pulling Rhetta out of her musings and back to the moment.

"Thank you so much, Edith. I'm so grateful to you for doing this."

"My pleasure, Rhetta. Have a delightful day." The woman winked at her, as though Rhetta was heading out for a lover's liaison, not taking Lee with her to interrogate a man who had answers to her questions, even if he refused to admit it.

Lee picked up the basket in one hand, munching on a piece of dried beef he held in the other. Rhetta opened the door, and the two of them walked outside into the bright sunlight and headed toward Milton's livery. Rhetta had asked R.C. yesterday if she could rent a buggy for the day. He'd assured her he'd have it ready for her when she arrived.

After waving to Anne who was outside gathering clothes off the line, Rhetta paid R.C. and climbed into the buggy he had hitched to a beautiful black horse he called Raven. Lee set the picnic basket in the back and slid onto the seat beside Rhetta, then she snapped the lines.

It took less than an hour to reach Rowan's ranch. On the way there, Lee was silent, observing the landscape filled with raw beauty. When she turned off the road onto Rowan's lane, Lee grinned and pointed to the herd of red and white cattle grazing in a pasture with grass nearly up to their knees.

"Are these Mr. Reed's cows?" Lee asked, studying the sturdy-appearing bovines.

"Yes, I believe so."

"They are a handsome bunch." Lee swiveled from staring at the cows to her. "Can you call cows handsome?"

"I don't see why not, although cows are females and bulls are the males. They aren't exactly pretty, but handsome is a fine word."

She saw movement on the porch of Rowan's house and hoped it wasn't his ill-behaved dogs waiting to twist her skirts into a knot. Honestly, the animals had just been rambunctious in their greeting, nothing else. They hadn't growled or barked or been threatening in any way. It was as though racing around her skirts was their way of welcoming her. Which was more than she could say for their standoffish owner.

As she pulled on the reins and Raven stopped, she glanced up to see Rowan glowering at her. Despite the sour look on his face, he was even more handsome than she recalled. His hair was a rich shade of brown that gleamed in the sunlight. He had scruff on his cheeks and jaws, like he hadn't shaved since Sunday, when she'd seen him sneaking out of church immediately after the service ended. His chin was stubbornly set, but his lips were full. She couldn't help but wonder what it would be like to kiss them.

"Terrible. It would be terrible," she muttered to herself, earning a concerned look from Lee as he hopped out of the buggy, then gave her a hand. She stepped down and brushed at her skirt, then froze at the sound of the dogs barking.

The two canines raced around the corner of the house, amid a cacophony of woofs. She braced for the impact of them running into her.

"Sit!" Rowan commanded, and both dogs sat at Lee's feet, tails wagging so hard, they fanned the dirt and stirred up puffs of dust.

"May I pet them, sir?" Lee asked, holding up both hands like he wasn't sure how to go about petting them.

Had Lee ever petted a dog? Surely, he had, although Rhetta couldn't recall when or where it might have happened.

Gracious. How many ways had she failed Lee as a parent? He'd always been so easy to care for, never making demands or whining or acting out, other than the few fights at school. She realized there were many things she should have done for him that she hadn't.

He'd never gone hungry. Always had clothes to wear and a warm roof over his head, and she'd poured out affection on him, but she'd never asked if he might have wanted a pet. Even if she didn't have time to bother with the care of a dog, she could have gotten him a cat.

“Let them sniff your hands, and then you can,” Rowan said, coming down the steps. He never even looked Rhetta’s way as he hunkered down by his dogs as they sniffed Lee’s fingers. “You must be Miss Wallace’s son, Lee.”

The boy nodded, dropped to his knees, then gingerly placed a hand on the larger of the two dogs.

Rowan rubbed his hand over the head and along the back of the other dog. When he scratched behind the animal’s ears, she flopped down and rolled onto her back, tongue lolling out in pleasure.

Lee tried the same with the second dog. It rolled onto his back and lifted his chin. Lee scratched beneath it and the dog closed his eyes, like he had found a place of bliss.

“What are their names?” Lee asked, looking at Rowan with a bit of hero worship in his expression.

Well, that would not do. At all. Rhetta fought the urge to pull Lee to his feet, shove him into the buggy, and leave before he got any wild notions about becoming friends with their prime suspect.

However, that would accomplish nothing beyond infuriating Lee and isolating them from the man she was determined to get to open up to them.

“The one you’re petting is Buck, and this silly girl is Kitty, his sister,” Rowan explained. “They’ve never been separated from each other.”

“Really?” Lee asked. “Is that common?”

Rowan shrugged. “I reckon that depends on the dogs and the situation and who owns them.” He gave Kitty a few more scratches, stood, and turned to Rhetta. "To what do I owe the pleasure of this visit?"

The way he said pleasure made it sound like something vile had settled on his tongue and he needed to spit it out.

Rhetta didn't meet his gaze. Instead, she fussed with the fingers of her gloves, snugging them down one at a time. "It was such a pretty day, we thought you might be interested in going on a picnic with us."

"A picnic?" Rowan asked, eyeing her like she'd lost her mind.

Her eyes met his, grateful he at least was fully clothed today. His shirt and denims were dusty, his knees stained with grass, and his boots coated in all manner of filth. Even so, he was still one of the most handsome men Rhetta had ever seen. Truthfully, Rhetta found him to be far better looking than the senator, although there certainly was a strong resemblance between the two men.

"A picnic. Mrs. Piedmont filled a basket for us to share," Rhetta said, waving a hand toward the large basket in the back of the buggy.

"You don't say," Rowan said, eyeing the basket with the same hunger she all too often recognized in Lee's expression.

"Would you have time for lunch with us, sir?" Lee asked, giving Rowan a hopeful look that only a heartless miscreant could have refused.

Rowan glanced at the basket again. "I reckon I can make a little time."

Lee grinned over his shoulder at Rhetta. "Hear that, Mama? We're going on a picnic with Mr. Reed."

She nodded and motioned to the buggy behind her. "Would you care to go somewhere for our picnic, or do you prefer to eat here?"

Rowan looked from her to the hem of her skirt. He possessed the audacity to grab ahold of her skirt and lift the fabric until he could see her shoes. As though that provided a suitable answer, he dropped her skirt and walked over to the buggy without a word. Rhetta battled the increasing desire to deliver a resounding whack to his head with her parasol.

"I'll drive the horse down to the barn, so he'll be in the shade and have water while we're eating," he said nonchalantly, as though he hadn't just behaved with complete impropriety. "Stay here."

Without waiting for her response, he handed her the picnic basket, slid onto the buggy seat, and drove down to the barn below them.

From this vantage point on a slight hill, Rowan had a wonderful view of his cattle grazing in the distance.

She turned and watched him jogging toward them. She hadn't given a thought to him being busy with his own work. Were they interrupting his day? Would he work into the evening darkness to catch up on the time they cost him with their unplanned visit?

Perhaps they could do something to assist him after they'd eaten.

Rowan didn't appear the least bit winded when he reached them. "Just give me one more minute," he said and charged onto the porch in two long strides, then disappeared inside the house. It wasn't overly large but appeared to be well constructed. She wondered if he'd built it himself. It wouldn't surprise her if he had. Rowan Reed may be hiding his past, but he did seem to be a capable, hardworking man.

Only a few minutes had passed before he emerged with a quilt tucked under one arm and another basket held in his hand. He'd settled a hat on his head, and Rhetta felt a small pang of regret that he'd covered up all that thick, shiny hair.

"Are you up for a little walk?" he asked, directing the question to Rhetta.

She nodded, grateful she'd worn sturdy boots instead of fashionable shoes. She'd also foregone her bustle today, opting for a plain dark blue skirt with a blue calico shirtwaist she had purchased from the mercantile in Holiday, wanting to fit in with the women who dressed not for showing off the latest fashions but for practical work.

Rowan held out the arm with the quilt, indicating a path that led into the trees behind his house. "Just follow me."

Anywhere.

Shocked, Rhetta glanced around to see where the voice had come from, then realized it was the one in her own head. Stupid voice. What did it know anyway?

Chapter Eight

Rowan had figured Miss Rhetta Wallace wouldn't give up easily. The fact that she'd come bearing food attested to her determination to win him over then coax a confession out of him. She'd even brought her son along, presumably to make her appearance today seem like a neighborly visit.

Well, it wasn't going to work. He had nothing to confess, and the last person he'd tell if he did was a detective hired by Senator Tomlinson. The man was a disgusting, detestable despot.

The boy, Lee, though, seemed intelligent and eager to learn all he could about life in the country. As Rowan led the way to an ideal picnic spot, Lee peppered him with questions about his cattle, the dogs, the ranch, and the work it entailed.

Rowan had noticed the boy wore cowboy boots and denims that appeared new. He wondered if Lee's interest was a phase the lad was passing through, or if he was genuinely enthralled with life in the West.

"Did any pioneers travel through here, Mr. Reed?" Lee asked as they hiked upward on the trail Rowan followed.

"Not from the Oregon Trail. We're a little too far east, but the trail goes right past Baker City. If you know where to look, you can stand in the wagon ruts. There are still people using that trail today although more and more people are traveling by train, or at least following the train tracks." Rowan glanced back to see Rhetta leaning forward, one hand carrying the picnic basket, the other trying to hold up her skirts so they didn't tangle in the brush.

"Maybe you should grab that basket from your mother," Rowan suggested.

Lee darted back to Rhetta, took the basket from her, and offered her his arm. The boy had nice manners. Rowan would give him that.

"Did you come by train or wagon, Mr. Reed?" Lee asked as they continued along the path.

"Both. I took a train part of the way. Spent time working at various ranches, traveling from one place to the next before I boarded the train and found myself in Baker City. I bought Buddy from a horse breeder in Texas, and he's been with me through many adventures."

"Buddy? That's your horse?" Lee asked. "What kind of horse is he?"

"The best kind," Rowan said with a grin over his shoulder, his eyes meeting Rhetta's once again. She might be a thorn in his side, but she was sure a pretty one. His grin widened into a genuine smile, admiring the way she filled out her flowered shirtwaist.

"Gracious!" Rhetta stumbled over a tree root and would have fallen if Lee hadn't held her upright.

Rowan ignored her near-fall and engaged in a conversation with Lee about the fine points of various horse breeds and what to look for when purchasing a horse.

The lad was smart but seemed to know nothing about animals of any type or what was required to live off the land or as part of it.

When they reached the spot Rowan had in mind for a picnic, Rhetta's face was flushed, making her pink cheeks even rosier. Her neatly styled hair was disheveled, with a curl plastered to her left cheek. He thought she looked far more appealing than she had in the fancy gown she'd worn on her previous visit to the ranch, or the stylish dresses she wore to church.

Yes, he'd made note of her sitting with Edith and Grover Piedmont and had purposely avoided her.

"Will this do?" he asked, turning to look at his guests. He'd led them to the top of the mountain behind his house, where he could see for miles and miles.

"It's incredible, Mr. Reed!" Lee said, his expression full of excitement. "I've never seen anything like this."

"Look all you like, Lee." Rowan said, slightly concerned by Rhetta's silence. She started to plop down on a rock, but he dropped the quilt, grabbed her arm, and pulled her to him.

When she looked like she was about to swat him, he pointed to a snake sunning itself on the rock.

"Is that a …?" Her voice trailed off, and she seemed slightly woozy. He fanned a hand in front of her face.

"Surely you aren't a woman given to fits of the vapors or fainting spells, are you, Miss Wallace? You don't strike me as the swooning type."

"I'm not, Mr. Reed." She straightened her spine, turned so her back was to the snake and looked out at the view. "It is wondrous up here, reptiles not included."

He chuckled softly. "It won't bother us if we leave it alone. Come on over here, far enough away from the snake so you won't have to worry about it sneaking up on you. Let's spread out the blanket and eat this lunch Edith packed for us."

Rowan released his hold on her arm, reluctantly. He rather liked her snugged up against his chest, even if he had a shirt covering it today.

He was man enough to admit he was smitten with Rhetta Wallace. What man wouldn't be? She was beautiful, smart, witty, and determined. But, at the moment, he viewed her as the enemy. Additionally, he had no plans to get entangled with a woman, so there was no point in pursuing his interest in her when nothing would come of it.

Rowan set down the basket he'd carried and picked up the blanket, spreading it out beneath the shade of a tree where they still had a grand view.

"May I assist you, Miss Wallace?" he said, holding out his hand to her as she walked over to the blanket.

The surprised look on her face made him think she expected his manners to be on par with a cavedweller, but he'd learned a few things over the years. She removed her gloves and hat, tossing them on a corner of the quilt, then settled her palm against his.

As soon as their hands connected, Rowan felt a jolt rock through him. He wasn't sure if he wanted to jerk his hand away or hold on tight and never let go.

Rhetta removed his need to make a decision when she quickly released his hand once she'd wrangled her skirts so she could take a seat. At least she'd left off the ridiculous bustle today. How any intelligent woman could wear all that padding fastened to her backside and expect to function normally was beyond his ability to understand.

Lee bounded over with the picnic basket, set it by Rhetta, then plopped onto the far end of the quilt, leaving Rowan to sit between the two of them.

Without a word, he folded his legs and took a seat, then reached into the basket he'd brought that held three jars full of water that had been cool when he'd pumped it from the kitchen sink. He handed one to Rhetta and the second to Lee before unscrewing the lid of the third and taking a drink. "It's just water."

"Thank you," Rhetta said, opening the jar and taking a dainty sip. The woman would die of dehydration if she didn't shake off her drawing room manners.

"Well, what did Edith pack for us to enjoy?" Rowan asked, watching as Rhetta opened the basket and extracted three plates with three napkins wrapped around cutlery.

The meal was better than he could have hoped, with crispy fried chicken, wedges of cheese, dill pickles, boiled eggs, and strawberry pie for dessert. The desserts the hotel served had vastly improved since Edith had started buying baked goods from Keeva Ryan. The pastor's wife liked to bake and had found a way to make money doing it.

The way John lived, willing to give anyone who needed it the shirt off his back, Rowan figured the young couple would need the money Keeva earned as well as her head for business. He'd noticed she was more than just a pretty face topped by a mass of flaming red hair.

John had chosen well when he'd picked her for his bride, even if she was quite young.

Rowan wondered, should the notion to marry ever settle over him, if he'd do as well as his friends in finding a wife who was a true partner to him.

For reasons he didn't care to examine, his thoughts shifted to Rhetta as she laughed at something Lee said. It lit up her whole face when she laughed, and her smiles, rare as they were in his presence, made her seem closer to Lee's age than Rowan's.

He suddenly found himself wanting to make her smile or laugh, to fill her with joy.

And that annoyed him.

He had no business warming up to the woman who had come to town to take away the life he'd worked so hard to build for himself. He'd spent years saving every penny he could, working for whoever would hire him, learning whatever anyone could teach him so he could one day own his own land. Be his own boss. Steer his future where he wanted it to go.

There was no way on this earth he'd walk away from the ranch without a fight.

However, today was a lovely day with a beautiful woman seated beside him, and a fine boy looking at him like he could be a hero. Today was for picnics and lightheartedness, not defending himself from a man who was, in Rowan's estimation, a heartless villain.

Once they'd finished eating and Lee had somehow found room to gobble up the last piece of strawberry pie, Rhetta packed the basket she'd brought with her, and he set the empty canning jars back in his basket.

Rowan gave Rhetta a hand as she rose elegantly from the quilt, prepared this time for the jolt that shot up his arm when their hands touched. He haphazardly folded the quilt and stuffed it into the basket with the jars, then waited as Lee and Rhetta took one more glance around at the breathtaking view. Rhetta pinned her hat back on her head and tugged on her dirty, damp gloves, and they started down the hill.

Lee swung the basket he carried and asked questions as they walked covering topics from the trees that grew on the hill to the variations in the seasons. When they returned to the house, Rowan sat his basket on the porch and turned to face his company.

"We've monopolized enough of Mr. Reed's time today, Lee. We should head back to town." Rhetta took the basket from Lee as he bent down to pet the dogs when they bounded off the porch to see him.

"I'll bring the buggy back around," Rowan said and hustled down to the barn where he'd parked the buggy in the shade and left a bucket of water for the horse to drink. It only took a few minutes before he stopped the buggy in front of where Lee and Rhetta stood, giving Kitty and Buck affectionate pats.

"If you aren't careful, they'll climb in the buggy and head home with you."

"I wouldn't mind," Lee said, grinning as he turned his head to keep from getting licked across the face by Kitty.

"I think Edith might take exception to the dogs in our room." Rhetta smiled indulgently, set the picnic basket into the buggy, then reached out a hand to Rowan. "Thank you for today, sir. It was a rare and memorable treat to dine with such a spectacular view."

He shook her hand, wondering what she'd do if he refused to let go. "It was my pleasure, Miss Wallace. Thank you for bringing a fine meal. I appreciated it."

She nodded, and then he helped her into the buggy with no choice but to release her hand once she was settled on the seat.

Lee hopped in beside Rhetta. "Thanks, Mr. Reed. I had a grand time."

Rowan nodded. An invitation for them to return next week lingered on his lips, but he held it in. The last thing he needed to do was encourage them to become friends.

He lifted a hand in parting as Rhetta snapped the lines and the horse started forward. It wouldn't do for him to get attached to the woman or her son. Not when he knew they'd be leaving soon, and especially when he knew the only reason Rhetta was trying to butter him up was to get him to talk.

Well, she'd have to do a lot more than bring a picnic lunch to loosen his tongue about his childhood.

But another strawberry pie and an afternoon sitting with Rhetta sure wouldn't hurt anything. Not a thing.

Chapter Nine

"Do you have plans today?"

The deep-timbred voice by her ear startled Rhetta. She jumped before she spun around and glared at Rowan. How he'd sneaked up on her, she had no idea. She hadn't even been aware he was still in the church yard. She'd assumed he'd ridden off right after the church service, as he'd done the past three Sundays.

"Plans, Miss Wallace? Do you have plans this afternoon?"

It was on the tip of her tongue to tell him she was busy, but she wouldn't lie. Besides, wasn't the whole point of her being in Holiday to get close enough to Rowan to wiggle a confession out of him? Since the day of the picnic at his ranch last week, she'd avoided him. It had felt too good, all too right, to be there with him and Lee, just enjoying a beautiful day without any ulterior motives at play.

In another time, another life, she could have easily fallen for Rowan Reed. He might be quiet and reserved, but he was kind. Thoughtful. Caring. Gentle. Yet, there was a strength in him that she thought might move mountains.

Lee had certainly been taken with him. For days, he'd talked about Mr. Reed this and Mr. Reed that until Rhetta wanted to pull out her hair. Or perhaps Rowan's. But his was so thick and rich, it would be a shame to destroy it.

This was precisely why she'd stayed away from him. She was attracted to him, more than she'd ever been to any man. She needed to sort out her personal feelings from her professional duties and finish this job. She'd received not one but three testy telegrams from Mr. Reynolds in the past week demanding to know if she'd found Reed Saunders.

She feared if she kept dragging her feet, Senator Tomlinson would send some of his hoodlums to investigate. If that happened, she had no doubt they'd injure or kill Rowan. The thought of that made her heart ache so badly, she could barely breathe.

"Are you well today, Miss Wallace?" Rowan asked, giving her a concerned look. "You seem upset."

Rhetta dragged her thoughts back to the moment and smiled at Rowan.

Mercy!

Why did he have to be so handsome? So brawny? So rugged and wonderful?

"I'm perfectly well, Mr. Reed. And to answer your question, I do not have plans for the afternoon. Lee and I discussed going for a walk this afternoon or perhaps renting a buggy and going for a drive."

"I was wondering if you'd like to come out to the ranch. We could eat lunch at the hotel first, unless you've grown tired of the food there."

"Hardly. The meals are delicious." Rhetta wanted to refuse to go to the ranch. To tell Rowan she wouldn't bother him again, but the sole reason she was in Holiday was to get him to tell her the truth. After weeks in town, she was no closer to discovering it now than she'd been when she arrived. Mr. Reynolds had assured her the senator was nearing the end of his patience with her. She had half a mind to tell the odious man she no longer cared to finish this job and the senator could keep his money.

The only thing that had prevented her from doing it was her desire to ensure financial stability for Lee's future.

Torn between doing what she was coming to view as the right thing or doing what she was under contract to finish, she found herself wavering in the middle, unable to move one way or the other.

She'd worry about that tomorrow.

Today, she'd been invited to join a handsome cowboy for lunch, and then a visit to his ranch. She could think of far worse ways to spend a Sunday afternoon.

"Is that a yes?" Rowan asked, giving her an encouraging grin. He'd taken the time to shave, and she found herself admiring his firm jawline and full lips. She hadn't noticed before, but he had a sprinkling of freckles on his nose that gave him a boyish appeal.

How could any woman resist such an endearing grin from such an appealing man?

"Yes. Lee will be elated. He's hardly spoken of anything but your ranch since our last visit."

Lee appeared at her side, his hair mussed and energy pulsing from him. "I heard my name."

"Yes, you did, darling boy. Mr. Reed has invited us to spend the afternoon at his ranch. Would you care to go?"

"Would I? That would be grand, Mama." He reached out and pumped Rowan's hand. "Thank you for inviting us, sir. Should I run to the livery and ask Mr. Milton if we can rent a buggy?"

"No need," Rowan said, motioning to a wagon pulled by a team of draft horses Rhetta hadn't even realized he owned. "If it suits you both, we can walk to the hotel and eat lunch, then if you wish to change before we go to the ranch, I can retrieve the wagon while you do so."

"That is a sound plan," Rhetta said, turning and heading in the direction of Main Street.

The hotel dining room wasn't overly busy, and they found a table in a back corner. Rowan and Lee ordered the same meal, and both chose lemon pie for dessert. Before he paid the bill, Rowan whispered something to their waiter, who returned with a small box that Rowan handed to Lee.

"Molasses cookies!" Lee said, shoving one into his mouth and closing the lid of the box. "Thank you, Mr. Reed."

"A boy needs plenty of sustenance." Rowan winked at Rhetta, and she felt heat spurt through her midsection. What was this man doing to her? Did she really want to know? No. She concluded she did not. At least not today.

"Thank you for lunch, sir. That was very kind of you to invite us to share it with you." Rhetta stood and motioned to Lee. "Come along, son. We'll change and meet Mr. Reed out front momentarily."

Lee handed Rowan the cookies, then fell into step beside her as they returned to their room.

Rhetta chose a raspberry pink cotton dress that she'd worn so many times, it was starting to fade, but it was one of her favorite dresses to wear when she was doing nothing more than studying files or enjoying a leisurely afternoon. She exchanged her dress shoes for the ankle boots she'd worn the last time she'd gone to the ranch, and her high-crowned hat for a straw hat that had seen better days. She didn't bother with gloves, knowing they'd be soggy and filthy before the afternoon was through. She grabbed her reticule and stepped out of her room to find Lee anxiously watching out the window in their sitting room.

"He just pulled up out front," Lee said, dashing for the door. Rhetta would have told him to walk instead of racing down the stairs, but he had so little fun in his life, so few opportunities for frivolity, that she wouldn't deprive him now.

Rowan jumped down from the wagon and motioned for Rhetta to walk over by him. She'd never climbed into such a tall conveyance and wasn't exactly sure where to begin. Rowan solved her dilemma by settling his hands on her waist and swinging her up to the seat.

A gasp rolled out of her as her hands wrapped around the hard muscles of his arms. Before she could take Rowan to task for handling her like a sack of feed, Lee scrambled up on the opposite side and bounced on the seat.

Rhetta swallowed her rebuke. She sat quietly as Rowan climbed onto the wagon, snapped the lines, and the horses plodded out of town.

Lee and Rowan carried the conversation with her son asking questions about everything from the plants growing on the side of the road to the birds flying overhead.

When they reached the ranch, Rowan offered them cool water from his well, then pointed to his saddle horse grazing in the pasture.

"I thought Lee might enjoy a riding lesson, if you approve, Miss Wallace."

Rhetta wanted to shake her head and protest. Lee might get hurt. What if the horse ran away with him? Or bucked him off? Or decided to trample him?

But the look on Lee's face forced her to hold back her fears and nod in agreement.

"I know it might be frightening for you, but Buddy is a safe mount, and I'll be right beside him," Rowan said, offering his assurance. "Everyone who lives in the West needs to know how to ride a horse."

Rhetta might have protested they didn't live in the West, but in Chicago, where they could walk most places they needed to go or hire a cab to take them. However, Rowan wasn't wrong. Riding a horse was a skill that would benefit Lee and one she was not capable of teaching him.

For the next hour, she leaned against the barn in the shade it provided and watched as Lee learned how to catch, saddle, and bridle a horse. Rowan showed him how to mount and dismount and gave him a lesson in how to get the horse to go, change direction and speed, and stop.

Finally, he turned the boy loose on Buddy. The horse walked at a sedate pace around the corral where the lesson had taken place.

"Look, Mama! I'm really riding."

"You really are, Lee. You're doing splendidly!"

Her son beamed at her, and she felt his joy all the way across the corral. She looked from him to Rowan, who stayed just a few feet away from the horse in case he needed to step in.

It was impossible for her to reconcile this kind, gentle giant to a wanted man who'd gunned down his best friend and run off before the law could catch him.

Rhetta decided before she asked Rowan more questions about his past, she would discuss her thoughts with two people she knew could offer sound advice.

Hours later, after Rowan had fixed them a simple meal of cold ham with leftover biscuits and fried eggs, they'd eaten the molasses cookies on the way back to town. He left them at the hotel with hardly a word of parting, other than to thank them for a nice afternoon.

Sleep eluded Rhetta as she thought over the afternoon spent at the ranch. Rowan was a good man. A man who deserved more than to be tossed into the clutches of a vengeful senator.

Regardless of what it might mean for her future, Rhetta waited until after she and Lee had enjoyed breakfast at the hotel the following morning to suggest he spend a little time with his friends before it got too hot out, then made her way to Pastor Ryan's home. She tapped on the door and smiled as Keeva yanked it open.

"Good morning, Rhetta. What brings you over so early in the day?" Keeva gave her a hug, then stepped back. "Not that you aren't welcome anytime."

Rhetta glanced behind her friend. "I was hoping your husband might have a few minutes to spare. I have a matter I'd like to discuss with him and Marshal Durant."

"Of course." Keeva reached out and squeezed her hand. "He's over at the church, but I'll send him to Dillon's office. If Dillon isn't there, he's likely on his way in from the farm."

Rhetta nodded, aware the marshal and Zara lived on a small farm just outside of town with the woman Dillon had adopted as his grandmother when he'd moved to Holiday. "Thank you, Keeva."

The woman squeezed her hand one more time. "Is there anything I can do?"

"Beyond prayers, no."

Keeva smiled. "You're already in my prayers, my friend."

Rhetta felt tears prickle her eyes, while her throat tightened. "Thank you," she mumbled, then turned and hurried toward the marshal's office.

She knocked on the frame of the screen door, then stepped inside to find Dillon Durant at his desk, looking through a stack of wanted posters.

He glanced up at the squeak of the door, then stood. "Good morning, Miss Wallace. How may I help you today?"

"There is a matter of importance I would like to discuss with you and the pastor. I, um … well, I could use your advice on how to proceed and would appreciate it if the matter remained confidential."

"Of course," Dillon said, pulling out one of the two chairs by his desk.

Rhetta had barely settled onto the seat when the door squawked and John Ryan rushed inside. His hair was a tousled mess, and it looked as though he'd rushed to tuck in his shirt, but he nodded at Rhetta and shook the marshal's hand before he took a seat beside her.

"Anything you tell us, Miss Wallace, won't be repeated," Dillon assured her. "What's happened?"

"I am a private detective." The shocked expression on the men's faces caught her off guard. Zara and Keeva had taken it to heart when she'd shared about her profession with them and asked them not to tell anyone.

"Well, that explains some things," Dillon said cryptically. "Please, go on."

Rhetta sat forward and placed the file she'd brought with her on Dillon's desk. She opened it and pointed to the photograph on top of the papers. "Senator Richard Tomlinson from Cincinnati contacted me in March. This is a photo of him with his son and wife. He said a man named Reed Saunders shot his son, then disappeared. He's been searching for twelve years for that man. He's hired numerous detectives over the years. The last sighting of him was in Texas several years ago. I took the job, realizing the senator was not forthcoming with certain details about the case, but I wanted to discover the truth. The funds he offered for the job were, frankly, impossible for me to refuse. They'll make it possible for me to send Lee to college."

"Reed Saunders? You think he's here? In Holiday?" the pastor asked.

"He's here." Dillon handed John the photo.

"Oh," John said, looking crestfallen.

"There is an undeniable resemblance between the senator and the man he says is Reed Saunders. I realized right away Reed is his son." Rhetta relayed the story about the harlot, the shooting, and her travels to track Reed to Holiday.

"I can see your dilemma. Rowan doesn't strike me as a cold-blooded killer." Dillon glanced at John, who nodded in agreement.

"But there is no doubt he is related to the senator. They simply look far too much alike for it to be a coincidence. After being here and spending time with Mr. Reed, I'm convinced he was, at some point in his past, Reed Saunders. But I'm also convinced he did not shoot Ricky Tomlinson. He told me he'd never killed anyone, and I believe him. However, the senator has grown impatient. He knows I'm here in Holiday and I fear it is only a matter of time before he sends his associates to deal with Rowan."

"I'll send a telegram today and see if I can get more information about the shooting. I know a few people who can make discreet inquiries," Dillon said, stuffing the information he'd looked through back into the file. He jotted down a few pertinent details with names and dates, then glanced at the pastor.

John took Rhetta's hand in his, then held one out to Dillon. With their hands joined, he prayed for them to have wisdom and ears that were open to the Lord's leading.

Rhetta added her own prayer that her actions wouldn't lead to harm befalling a good man.

"Thank you," she said, rising to her feet, then picked up the file that seemed to grow heavier by the day and returned to the hotel to wait.

Chapter Ten

Rowan glanced at the sun and sighed. It couldn't have been more than five minutes since the last time he'd checked its progress across the sky. Rhetta had lingered in his thoughts all day and caused him to be distracted.

Try as he might, he'd been unable to roust her out of his mind. Not that he really wanted to banish all thoughts of the beautiful, intriguing woman. He'd pieced together enough of what she'd shared to know she'd come at the behest of Senator Tomlinson to verify he was Reed Saunders and let the man know his whereabouts. He had assumed that by now Dillon would have ridden out to the ranch and hauled him into town in handcuffs.

Yet, when he'd seen the marshal at church on Sunday, he'd greeted him with the warmth of a friend.

Regardless, Rowan had that feeling he got whenever something terrible was about to happen. It had been plaguing him since Rhetta and Lee had arrived in town. The only tragedy that had occurred, as far as he could tell, was him falling in love with the woman who was sent to turn him over to the senator.

Why couldn't she have been an old, ugly hag? Or some dimwitted, twitterpated girl? Why did she have to be so intelligent, witty, resourceful, and determined, not to mention incredibly lovely?

Rhetta Wallace was exactly the type of woman he would marry if he were inclined to enter that sacred union. Sure, she had no idea which end of a cow to milk or how to gather eggs or even tend a garden. He wasn't convinced she knew how to boil water, but he didn't care. Those were things she could learn in time if she chose.

What she already knew was how to be a good mother and a loving, tender, caring person.

If Rowan cared to admit it, he was as fond of Lee as he was of Rhetta. The boy was smart, clever, quick to learn, and interested in the world around him. He was mannerly and thoughtful and protective of his mother. Although Rowan had never given any thought to having a family of his own, he sure wouldn't mind Rhetta for his wife and Lee for his son.

He held a hand up to his ear, but it came away dry. Apparently, all his brains weren't yet leaking out his ears, but they had to be close for marriage to even enter his mind.

Rowan knew he was just dreaming big dreams. He could dream all he wanted about Rhetta and Lee living on the ranch with him, but it wasn't meant to be. Not as long as the senator insisted on holding him accountable for something he didn't do.

With his thoughts tumbling over themselves, he'd been as worthless as a shirt missing all its buttons this afternoon.

He gave up on work and saddled Buddy. After a dip in the creek to clean away the labors of his day, he returned to the house and pulled on clean clothes, took a few coins from the stash he kept hidden in his bedroom, and headed into town.

The urge to see Rhetta was strong, so he figured he might as well ask her if he could join her and Lee for supper at the hotel.

If he ate there with any more frequency, Edith might start charging him rent for a room, mistaking him for a guest.

He tied Buddy to a hitching rail in the shade across from the hotel, walked inside, and glanced around the lobby. Rhetta wasn't there, so he approached the front desk where Edith sorted through the day's mail.

"Howdy, Edith," he said, leaning an arm on the counter.

"Evening, Rowan. What brings you to the hotel?" she asked innocently, then grinned at him and pointed toward the dining room. "She just went in there a few minutes ago."

"Thank you," Rowan touched the brim of his hat and politely tipped his head, then strode across the lobby to the dining room. He removed his hat and spied Rhetta sitting at a table by a window with a book spread open in front of her. At least she wasn't studying that file full of his past.

He waited until he stood on the opposite side of the table to clear his throat. She jumped and glanced up at him with a scowl that slowly lifted into a smile.

"Mind if I join you?"

"I'll have to consider it," she said, and tapped her chin, pretending to weigh the decision. "Dining alone since Lee is off with one of his friends enjoying a mess of fish the boys caught or suffering through a meal with one such as yourself." She closed the book and slid it to the edge of the table. "I think I shall somehow endure a meal with your insufferable presence."

"Insufferable, now, am I?" Rowan asked, setting his hat on the empty chair beside him. "Is that a step up or down from incorrigible?"

"Up, I think." Rhetta grinned at him, and his heart pounded out a beat that felt like a runaway horse galloped in his chest.

Throughout the meal, their conversation was lively, discussing articles they'd read in the newspaper. Rhetta had an opinion on every topic he brought up, and he took opposing views just to watch her blue eyes flash as she defended her position and thoughts.

"You're terrible," she said after the waitress cleared away their plates. "You can't convince me you are in favor of a tax on cattle."

A grin he tried to hide behind his glass of lemonade made his cheek twitch. When he set the glass on the table, she swatted his arm with her napkin. "You should never play cards with Henley Holt."

"Why, beyond the fact that she was raised by a professional gambler?" Rowan leaned back wondering what fascinating thing Rhetta would next say.

"Because your cheek twitches and you glance to your left when you aren't being truthful."

"Is that so?" Rowan asked. No wonder he'd always been terrible at playing poker. He used to think it was just bad luck. After he opened his heart to Jesus, he'd stopped playing cards for money, but occasionally, he played just for fun.

"It is so." Rhetta stood, and Rowan hopped up from his seat.

"I'll return in a moment. Please finish your lemonade."

He watched her walk from the room, her skirts swishing just enough for the room to feel as though Edith was pumping the heat from the kitchen oven directly over him. He gulped what was left of his lemonade and left money on the table for the meals, as well as a tip for the waitress who looked overheated and weary. When he saw Rhetta in the doorway, he hurried over to her.

"Would you like to go for a stroll?"

"That would be nice," she said, placing her hand on his arm as he held open the hotel door and walked outside with her.

If anyone had told him six months ago that he'd be so besotted with a woman that he'd abandon his work and spend his evening squiring her around town, he'd have told them they were crazy.

But here he was, meandering along Main Street with Rhetta on his arm while a dozen chores he'd intended to get to today went ignored. At the moment, he didn't even care. All he wanted was to spend more time with Rhetta. He had a feeling his days as a free man were growing short, and he just didn't have it in him to pack up and run again. Not when he'd finally found a home in Holiday.

Maybe that was what felt so different this time. Before, when he'd packed up and run anytime a detective had started snooping around, he hadn't left behind anyone who cared, except for Preacher Bill. Now, he had friends. True friends. He had the ranch he'd worked so hard to save enough money to buy. He had a life he'd come to appreciate and savor.

If he somehow ended up dead or in prison for whatever imaginary crimes the senator tossed at him, he'd written out his wishes and left them with Pastor Ryan. The man, young as he was, could be trusted to carry out his wishes. Of that, Rowan had not a single doubt.

For now, though, he just wanted to enjoy this time with Rhetta.

Rather than continue walking through Holiday with eyes watching them, he guided her out of town to the river, where they could have a little more privacy. Not that he planned to do anything that required privacy, but Rowan was a private man. He hadn't felt comfortable around people for a dozen years.

He guided Rhetta to a shady spot where they could sit on a fallen log and watch the water as it rushed along.

"This is pretty. Lee has mentioned the river, but I haven't come out here for a walk." Rhetta turned to him. "Thank you for thinking of it. It has to be ten degrees cooler here than in town."

He nodded in agreement. "It is cooler, and quieter."

Rhetta studied him for a long moment. He could see she wanted to ask him something, but she hesitated.

Trust didn't come easy for Rowan, but if he couldn't trust the woman he loved, he figured he couldn't trust anyone. He took Rhetta's hand and held it in his. Her skin so light and delicate against his tanned, work-roughened palm.

"Your hands are so big. Like paws," she teased, wrapping both of her hands around his and lifting it until she could kiss the back of it. "I bet if you grew out your hair and beard, you might look like a big grumpy bear."

"Grumpy bear? Why, I ought to toss you in the water for insulting me like that," he said with mock affront.

She went from a happy, playful countenance to appearing concerned, until she looked into his eyes and realized he was teasing.

He thought she might swat at him again, but she kissed the back of his hand a second time, then settled with their joined hands resting on her thigh.

"This is so nice, Rowan. Thank you."

"It is nice," he said, wanting to slide around behind her and pull her to rest against his chest so he could bury his face in her fragrant hair. Instead, he looked out at the water for a while, letting the silence soothe him.

Finally, he glanced at Rhetta, and found her studying him again. A long pent-up breath blew out of his mouth along with the last of his resistance to this incredible woman God had brought into his life.

"Rhetta, ask me again that question you asked the first day you came to the ranch."

She appeared confused, then stiffened slightly. "Today? Don't you just want to enjoy this lovely evening?"

"I do, but I want you to know the truth."

"Fine, then. Are you Reed Saunders?" she whispered the question so quietly, Rowan wouldn't have heard her if he hadn't been sitting so close to her.

"I used to be." He cleared his throat. "My name is Rowan Reed Saunders."

"Tell me, Rowan. Tell me your story," she pleaded, gently squeezing the hand that held hers.

"Part of the senator's story isn't fiction. My mother was a working girl. He was one of her clients. When she realized she was expecting, she couldn't bring herself to do anything drastic, so she basically went into hiding, working in the brothel's kitchen until I was born. I spent the first eight years of my life living in a brothel. The girls were all like aunts to me. It was an unusual childhood, for certain. I had a little room off the kitchen, next to where the cook slept. I did chores around the place in the mornings. Then I had school in the afternoon taught by my mother and two other girls. The evenings, after the kitchen was cleaned up, I went to my room and stayed there. I was only allowed to play outside in the mornings when the business was closed."

"It doesn't sound terrible," Rhetta said, "although it was a horrid place to raise a child."

Rowan nodded. He wouldn't elaborate on all the things he'd seen and heard no child should be exposed to. His mother had done the best she could, but it hadn't been enough.

"I'd just turned eight when a truant officer showed up one day, insisting I be allowed to attend school. My mother wasn't in a position to argue with him, so I went. I loved learning and being around other children, something I'd never been able to do much before then. That very first day, I met Ricky, and we became immediate friends. He just seemed to understand me, as I did him. Students and teachers got us confused all the time, and it made no sense to us. One day, we were playing after school and looked at our reflections in a window. We looked enough alike to be twins, except Ricky was dressed in the finest clothes money could buy, and I wore clothes that were a size too small or too big, depending on what donation box my mother had dug them out of."

"What did you think, when you realized you had to be brothers?" Rhetta asked quietly.

Rowan recalled all the feelings he'd experienced. "We couldn't believe it could be true, but the proof was in our faces. We shared the same father. Ricky wasn't mad about it. He had no siblings and was excited I was his brother. I finally asked my mother about it, and she turned so pale, I thought she might die. She started yelling at me that I didn't have a father and I never would and to get the idea out of my head. The first time Ricky invited me to his house to play after school, I wanted to go to meet the senator. To see the man I thought was my father. Ricky had gone to his room to get a ball and left me in the parlor. The senator walked in and thought I was Ricky, then he realized his mistake. I've never seen anyone look as furious as he did in that moment."

"Did he hurt you? Strike you?"

"No, but he forbade Ricky from bringing me to his house again or playing with me. He even sent Ricky to a boarding school, but Ricky started running away and coming to find me, so he gave up and sent Ricky back to school with me. I was allowed to visit Ricky's home, but every time I went, my mother looked like she was terrified it would be the last time she saw me, and his mother refused to be in the same room with me. Out of the blue one day, my mother inherited a house and a little money from a client. For me, it was the best gift in the world because I finally got to live in a house, even though it was little more than a shack. It meant my mother no longer worked at the brothel, and I didn't have to be mortified if someone asked for my address at school."

Rowan wondered if he'd ever told his mother how much it had meant to him when she'd moved to that house. She'd taken in mending and laundry and worked as a dishwasher at a restaurant for a while just to have money to keep food on the table. It had been hard on her, but she'd done it for him.

"When I was fifteen, Ricky's father gave him a pistol as a gift. There was a group of us in the park by Ricky's house, acting stupid like boys that age are prone to do. Ricky was showing off, although none of us knew how to shoot the pistol. Honestly, I didn't even know it was loaded. I don't know exactly what happened, but Ricky accidentally pulled the trigger and shot himself in the heart. He died instantly. I'd dropped beside him, placed my hand over the wound trying to staunch the flow of blood, begging him not to die. One of the boys went to fetch his mother, who started screaming and wouldn't stop. By the time the senator arrived, I was nearly as hysterical as Mrs. Tomlinson. Ricky wasn't just my best friend. He was my brother. My brother."

"How could the senator blame you for something that was clearly an accident?" Rhetta asked, her face full of sorrow and questions. "Something that was witnessed by others?"

"Even though the gun was still in Ricky's hand, the senator needed it to be someone's fault, so he shouted at the police to arrest me. While he'd adored Ricky, he loathed my very existence. The only one who despised me more was his wife. I could see the hatred in her eyes every time she looked at me because I was a reminder of the senator's philandering ways."

"Did they take you to jail?"

Rowan nodded, remembering the night he'd spent in a cold jail cell, covered in his brother's blood. "The next morning, the sheriff came and let me go. He took me to a bathhouse to clean up and bought me a new set of clothes. Then he took me to a café to eat. He asked me questions until I told him every detail of not just the shooting, but of why the senator and his wife hated me. After that, he patted me on the shoulder, told me to go home to my mother, and promised I wouldn't go to jail."

Rowan stopped and glanced out at the water again, needing a minute to gather his composure.

"You don't have to tell me more, Rowan, unless you want to." Rhetta offered him a look not of pity, but of understanding, and it gave him the courage to finish the story.

"I went home and found Arietta—that was my mother's name and what I'd always called her—had packed a bag for me. She told me if I wanted to live, I had to leave. She admitted then that the senator was my father and a horrible man, and he wouldn't stop until I was in jail or dead. She gave me all the money she had, kissed both of my cheeks and hugged me so tightly I thought I might suffocate, then she pushed me out the door. One of the girls from the brothel was waiting with a rented buggy and drove me to the train station. She handed me a ticket and told me she had a brother in Boston I could stay with for a while."

"But the senator tracked you there. You were only there a month before you went to New York, then Virginia, Texas, Kansas, and back to Texas," Rhetta said. He'd known she'd gleaned the history of his traveling from all the places the senator had tracked him.

Rhetta's brow furrowed, and she tightened her hold on his hand. "What happened to your mother?"

"I don't have proof, but I'm fairly certain she was murdered when she refused to tell anyone where I went." Rowan's mother might not have been a good example, but she had loved him in her own way and done her best to protect him. "The senator couldn't accept the fact that Ricky had accidentally killed himself, so I became the villain in the story. He told anyone who would listen how a boy raised in debauchery grabbed the gun he'd gifted to his son and shot him out of raging jealousy."

"Why is he still after you, Rowan? What does he hope to accomplish after all these years?" Rhetta asked with tears in her eyes. "What happened to the boys who saw what really happened?"

"Those boys all told the truth to the police. The sheriff had all the reports. That's why my face never ended up on a wanted poster. I don't know what happened to the sheriff. I'm sure the senator probably had him fired, but he knows the truth, and now, so do you."

Rhetta leaned forward and kissed Rowan's cheek. "Thank you for telling me. For entrusting me with your story."

He nodded and brushed away the tears lingering on her face with the pads of his thumbs. Her skin was as silky as he'd imagined. All he wanted was to hold her, to kiss her, to lose himself in the comfort he knew he'd find with her. But he couldn't.

Not as long as the senator still wanted his head on a platter.

"Why didn't you just face the senator and force him to admit he's been lying all these years," Rhetta asked.

Rowan scoffed. "If you were a judge, would you believe Senator Tomlinson with all his money and power and years in office or a scruffy cowhand who's been on the run his entire adult life?"

Rhetta nodded. "It's too bad no one knows what happened to the sheriff. I asked when I started searching for you. It's like he just disappeared."

"Or was made to disappear." Rowan stood and pulled Rhetta up beside him. "I should get you back before it gets dark. Lee will be returning to the hotel, ready to brag about all the fish he caught and ate."

Rhetta smiled, as he'd known she would. "I don't know where he puts all that food. There are times I'm not even sure he chews but just inhales it right off his plate."

Rowan chuckled and wrapped his arms around her, giving her a hug. "Thank you," he whispered and kissed her temple.

Before she could ask questions, he took her hand in his and headed back into town. Rhetta must have felt the need for silence as much as he did. He'd bared his soul to her, and she'd let him. They both had a lot to think over and consider.

He walked her inside the hotel's lobby, kissed her fingertips, tipped his hat to Edith, and left.

All he could do now was wait and see if Rhetta was the kind of person he sincerely hoped her to be.

Chapter Eleven

"Mama, if you don't stop pacing, you're going to wear a hole clean through that carpet, and Mrs. Piedmont won't be happy about that."

Rhetta turned and looked at Lee as he sat on an overstuffed chair with an apple fritter in one hand and a piece of cheese in the other. They'd eaten lunch an hour ago, but Lee had wanted a snack.

While he ate, she'd resumed the pacing she'd done all morning following a night spent tossing in her bed.

After Rowan had told her his story yesterday, her heart had hurt so badly for the little boy who'd lived in a brothel, for the child who had desperately wanted a brother he couldn't claim, for his rejection from a man who not only hated him but hunted him like an animal. It was no wonder Rowan had come to Oregon and hidden himself away in the town of Holiday. The senator would likely have never thought to look for him way out west like this if Rhetta hadn't been so determined to find Reed Saunders and discover the truth.

At the moment, she regretted sharing what she had with the pastor and marshal. What if the marshal's inquiries were intercepted by some of the senator's people? What if he sent some of his hired bullies to kill Rowan?

Knowing the senator, though, he would want the satisfaction of doing that himself. Rhetta wondered if the man had killed Rowan's mother just because he could.

The whole thing was such a terrible tragedy that didn't have to be. She couldn't even begin to fathom the pain that would rip through her if something happened to Lee. However, the senator still had Rowan. He could have shared his grief with his living son, but instead, he focused only on the one who was gone.

What had she done? What if her pursuit of the truth ended with a good man locked behind bars or dead?

Perhaps she should go talk to Dillon again, tell him what she'd learned. Beg him to protect Rowan if the need arose. Surely if a marshal were on Rowan's side, the courts would listen, wouldn't they?

"Mama!" Lee's voice cut through her turmoil. "What is going on? Why are you so upset?"

Rhetta started to deny that she was and couldn't. She took the seat across from Lee's and sighed. "I think I've done a terrible thing."

Lee set down his food and leaned forward, taking her hands in his. When had they gotten as big as the rest of him? She recalled how small his little fingers had looked the first time he'd let her hold his hand.

Rhetta wasn't ready for him to grow up and become a man. When he did, she'd be all alone again. More than that, though, she couldn't protect him if she wasn't with him.

She looked from his hands to his face that was starting to fill out more. The good-looking boy he was now would one day become a handsome man. A man she hoped would be good and kind, and true.

"What did you do, Mama, that you think is terrible? You're the best person I know, so it can't be that bad."

She smiled at him and squeezed his hands. "I think it was a mistake to take this case. Rowan is a good person, and the senator hasn't told the truth about the circumstances regarding his son's death. He lied to the authorities. He's lied all these years. I'm afraid he means to do great harm to Rowan. Because of me, he knows Rowan is here."

"You sent a telegram telling them Rowan is Reed Saunders? Why would you do that?" Lee jerked his hands from hers.

She grabbed his hands in hers to keep him from leaping away from her. "I didn't send a telegram, darling boy. I believe my attempts at stalling the inevitable have likely drawn their suspicions. I haven't heard from Mr. Reynolds in more than a week, and that doesn't bode well considering the number of telegrams he's been sending."

"Oh." Lee sank back into his chair. "That's bad, isn't it?"

Rhetta nodded.

"What can we do to help? Can we help Rowan pack? I could feed the animals if he needs to leave."

Rhetta feathered her fingers through Lee's hair. "It's not that simple, son. Rowan is tired of running. He's set down roots here in Holiday and wants to stay."

"Then we need to help him. If Marshal Durant knows the truth, he won't let them take Rowan, will he?"

"No, I don't expect he will."

Lee jumped up and tugged on her hands. "Then let's go tell him."

"I've already spoken with the marshal, and Pastor Ryan."

Lee smiled. "Then we don't need to worry. We've got the law and God on our side."

Rhetta couldn't help but grin at his logic. "Come on. Let's go for a walk. Rowan showed me the river. It's lovely. Is that where you boys fish?"

"Not most of the time. There's a creek we like to go to. I could show you."

"I'd like that." Rhetta settled a straw hat on her head and followed Lee down the stairs and out the door. They'd only walked part of the way down the block when she realized she'd forgotten her reticule. She thought it might be nice to go to the mercantile on their way back to the room and stop for a treat or maybe even get a new book to read.

"I forgot my reticule, Lee. I'll retrieve it and be right back." She turned to head back to the hotel and saw a man who looked like Mr. Reynolds striding down the boardwalk. She gave Lee a shove, and the two of them ducked into the alley.

"That sure looked like Mr. Reynolds," Lee said, his eyes wide and full of fear.

"I thought so. Before we panic, let's make certain it's him." Rhetta took Lee's hand, and they ran down the alley and along the back of the hotel. She tapped on the back door, and the chef opened it, recognizing them.

"What's happened?" he asked.

"I think Mr. Reed is in danger and need to be certain before I go to the marshal. May we sneak through the kitchen to the dining room?"

"Certainly, Miss Wallace." The chef walked them through the kitchen, and she nodded her thanks to him at the door into the dining room. The business was closed for the afternoon before the dinner service began, so she and Lee rushed to the entry door and carefully pushed it open. Together, they peeked around the edge of it and saw Edith speaking to a man who looked like Mr. Reynolds. When he asked after Rhetta's whereabouts, she knew they were all in trouble.

Silently, she closed the door, then turned to Lee. "Listen to me, son. I want you to go back through the kitchen, run down the alley, and don't stop until you get to the marshal's office. If he isn't there, go to Pastor Ryan. Tell them trouble from Cincinnati has arrived and Rowan needs help."

"What are you going to do, Mama?" Lee gave her a frantic look.

"I'm going to ride out to Rowan's ranch. Someone has to warn him."

Lee threw his arms around her and gave her a bone-cracking hug. "Be careful. You're the only mom I ever had, and I don't want to train a new one."

She smiled at his attempt at joking and patted his cheek. "I don't want to have to train another son. Be safe, darling boy. I love you."

"I love you, Mama."

Rhetta waited until Lee disappeared into the kitchen before she went back to the door and once again cracked it open. Mr. Reynolds was demanding to see her, and Edith looked like she was about to lose her patience with him.

Grover suddenly appeared with a shotgun and aimed it at Mr. Reynolds. "My wife asked you to leave. Unless you want to be carried out in pieces, I suggest you get to leaving."

Mr. Reynolds uttered several oaths, gave the Piedmonts withering glares, then slammed out the front doors.

Rhetta waited until he stormed down the street to run out of the dining room.

"Oh, thank heavens you're safe," Edith said, rushing around the front counter and giving Rhetta a hug. "Where's Lee?"

"I sent him to get the marshal. I'm going out to Rowan's place. We must warn him."

"Rowan? What's this got to do with that kind man?"

"That's not my story to tell, but his past is about to catch up to him, and we can't let that happen."

"Do you know how to ride?" Edith asked as she guided Rhetta through the dining room and kitchen to the back door.

"I understand the mechanics involved."

Edith rolled her eyes. "Good heavens. Don't break your neck, child. Ask one of the men to ride out there for you."

"Thank you, Edith, for being a lovely friend." Rhetta hugged her quickly, lifted her skirts, and took off at a run down the alley. She cut through two more before making her way to the livery.

"Well, Miss Rhetta. What can I do for you today?" R.C. asked as he looked up from shoeing a horse.

"I need a horse, R.C. One that won't buck me off because I've never ridden one before, but I must get to Rowan's place right away. His life is in danger."

R.C. set down the horse's foot held between his thighs and led the animal into a stall. He whipped off the leather apron he wore, and hastily saddled a powerful looking horse Rhetta knew she had no hope of controlling.

"Don't move," R.C. warned, then raced up a set of stairs that went to the apartment he and Anne shared above the livery. She heard him holler at Anne he had to be gone for a little while. When he returned, he had a gun holster around his hips and a rifle in his hands.

"What are you doing?" Rhetta asked as he led the horse outside and swung onto the back of it.

"Taking you to Rowan. He'd never forgive me if I let you break your neck getting there." R.C. waggled a hand at her. "Just grab on, and I'll do the rest."

Rhetta took his hand, and he swung her up behind him. She was glad she had on her favorite raspberry pink dress because the skirt was full, and she didn't have a bothersome bustle in her way.

Before Rhetta could do more than tighten her tenuous hold on R.C.'s waist, he clucked to the horse, and it thundered out of town.

Rhetta closed her eyes and held on, praying she wouldn't fall off. Praying they'd reach Rowan before his father found him. Praying she and Rowan would have a chance.

A chance?

Yes, that's what she wanted. A chance at love and happiness. A chance at a home and a family that included more than just her and Lee. A chance to show Rowan how much she admired him, needed him, cared for him. A chance to tell him how deeply she loved him.

Far faster than she would have imagined possible, she felt the horse turn and opened her eyes. They raced up Rowan's lane and skidded to a stop by the barn.

"Rowan!" R.C. bellowed, giving Rhetta a hand as she slid off the side of the horse. He hopped off and glanced around, but all was still and quiet. "Rowan!"

The sound of footsteps suddenly pounded toward them. Rowan appeared around the curve of the hill by the house and hastened toward them.

"What's wrong?" He looked from R.C. to Rhetta, then behind her, like he searched for Lee. "Where's Lee? Is he hurt? Are you hurt?" He took Rhetta's arms in his hands. "What's happened?"

"They're here. The senator's man is here. He was looking for me at the hotel. I sent Lee to get the marshal. R.C. kindly brought me out to warn you."

"Oh. I …" For a moment, Rowan looked like he might be ill. All the color faded from his skin.

Rhetta bracketed his face with her hands and pulled his head down until his forehead touched hers. "All will be well, Rowan. All will be well."

He drew in a deep breath, and when he raised his head, his face was once again tan, his jaw set with determination.

After a quick kiss to her temple, Rowan looked at R.C. and pointed to his rifle. "How good are you with that?"

"Almost as good as Grant Coleman."

Rowan grinned. "How about you get into a position in the barn loft? You'll be able to keep a good eye on things from there. I'll take Rhetta to the house."

"No." Rhetta set her feet when Rowan gave her hand a tug. "I'm not leaving you. If they come in here with their guns blazing, they can just shoot us both because I'm not leaving you." She twined her fingers around Rowan's. "I'm standing beside you."

"You'd better listen to the lady, Rowan. She sounds like she means business." R.C. smirked as he led his horse into the barn.

"Rhetta, it's not safe out here. Will you please go up to the house?"

"I will not." She fisted her hands on her hips. "Do I need to shout it for you to understand, you dense man? I'm not leaving you."

"Okay." Rowan spoke softly, then he wrapped an arm around her waist. "Okay," he said with more conviction.

"Just kiss her already!" R.C. hollered from the barn.

Rowan glowered in that direction before he leaned his head down so his lips brushed Rhetta's ear. "I've been dreaming for courage. Praying for courage. Pleading for the courage to tell you how I really feel, Rhetta. If something happens today, I want you to know I love you. I truly love you, and I want to spend whatever is left of my life with you."

"Oh, Rowan. I love you too. I love you more than you can imagine." She turned her head, so their lips were just a breath apart. "If something happens today, I don't want to spend my life wondering what it would have been like to have been kissed by you."

Rowan buried his hands in her hair. Until his fingers twined through it, she hadn't realized she'd lost her hat and most of her hairpins somewhere along the road. His hands slid down her back, and he rested them at her waist. He dropped his forehead to hers again for the length of a few heartbeats before he tugged her closer and his lips touched hers, so softly at first, she thought she imagined it.

Then his mouth moved on hers, tempting, coaxing, and soon they were both lost in a kiss more passionate than anything Rhetta had dreamed existed. She could have died with Rowan's lips locked to hers, but she wasn't ready to draw her last breath. The good Lord willing, no one would die today, but if the unthinkable happened, at least Rowan knew he was loved.

He pulled back and for a third time rested his forehead to hers before he took a step back, and in that instant, she saw him transform from the tender man who loved her to a tower of strength prepared to defend his home and loved ones.

Together, they went to the house and retrieved Rowan's pistols, shotgun, and rifle. He gave Rhetta a quick lesson in how to shoot and hold the rifle.

"I've shot a gun before," she said holding the weapon to her shoulder, getting accustomed to the weight of it.

"You've what?" Rowan asked, looking shocked.

"I bought a Derringer for protection and taught myself to shoot it. It's in my reticule back at the hotel. Had I known what today would bring, I certainly wouldn't have left without it."

Rowan gaped at her, then shook his head. "You are full of surprises today, Rhetta Wallace."

"I suppose I am." She pointed to a wide tree down past the chicken coop. "That would be a good place to hide, wouldn't it?"

"It would, but be careful. I don't need you getting shot when I finally found the woman I intend to spend the rest of my life loving."

She smiled and kissed his cheek. "I love you, Rowan. We will continue this conversation later."

"Yes, we will."

Rowan walked with her to the tree and made sure she was out of sight, then he whistled for the dogs and commanded them to stay with her. He gave her a quick kiss before he hid behind the shed where he kept the wagon and farm equipment.

When they heard hoofbeats coming down the lane, Rhetta felt her legs begin to tremble.

"Courage, don't you dare fail me now," she whispered to herself and held her position behind the tree.

"Reed! I know you're here. In fact, I'm sure that Rhetta Wallace is with you. Come out now and surrender, and no one has to die today." Rhetta recognized Senator Tomlinson's voice. She wondered where he'd been waiting while Mr. Reynolds had been at the hotel looking for her.

"We could smoke them out, boss. Set fire to the barn or the house." That was the voice of Mr. Reynolds.

If Rhetta hadn't been wearing her bright pink dress, she might have peeked around the tree to see how many men the senator had brought with him. She doubted he'd travel with only Mr. Reynolds for protection. Then again, too many of his hired guns would draw unwanted attention.

"I'll count to ten, Reed. If you haven't shown your face by then, I'll let my associate start burning down your place, one building at a time." Rhetta could almost picture the demented glee on the man's face as he spoke. What kind of monster could be so vengeful, especially to his own flesh and blood?

Rhetta felt sweat trickling down her back as she tried to remain motionless. She drew in a shallow breath a moment before a hand clapped over her mouth and another grabbed her around the waist. Before she could scream, the man spun her around and she looked into the face of Pastor Ryan. Behind him, Lee held a finger to his lips, motioning for her to remain quiet.

Rhetta nodded and the pastor released her.

"Reinforcements have arrived," Lee whispered in her ear. John pointed through the trees. She could see Josh Gatlin, the saddlemaker, Gordon Piedmont, and Rupert Rogers from the mercantile all armed and ready for action.

Rowan must have realized he wasn't alone because he stepped out from behind the shed with his hands upraised. "I'm here, Senator Tomlinson. No need for you and Mr. Reynolds to do anything drastic."

"Ricky," the senator said, swinging out of his saddle and taking a few steps toward him. For a moment, it seemed the man thought he was talking to his deceased son and not the one he intended to kill. He smiled and opened his arms wide.

Rowan continued toward him and stopped when he was just a few feet away. "No, Pa, it's me. Reed."

The smile melted off the senator's face. "Don't call me Pa. I may have fathered you, but that doesn't make you my son. You were never my son. You should have been the one to die, not my Ricky."

Rowan's face was expressionless, but Rhetta was certain he was trying to use the parental moniker as a way to provoke the senator into confessing the truth.

He shrugged. "Maybe, Pa. But you're the one who bought him that pistol without teaching him how to properly use it. We were just playing with it, and it went off. If you want to blame anyone for what happened, blame yourself, Pa."

The senator's face mottled with rage, and he took a swing at Rowan, slugging him in the stomach.

From her vantage point behind the tree, with Rowan facing her, Rhetta could see him clearly. He didn't wince or show the slightest change in his posture although the punch had to have hurt.

Despite the resemblance between the two men, Rowan was inches taller and wider than the senator. Looking at the two of them, she felt as though she was staring at a mirror image of good versus evil.

"I hate you, you worthless son of a harlot. You deserved to die, not Ricky. Not my boy. It drove his mother mad, knowing you lived and Ricky died. I told her not to. Told her to let it go, but she couldn't stand it. Couldn't stand knowing you even existed. She went to your mother, begged her to tell her where you were, but Arietta refused. So, she smothered her. Held a pillow over her face until she couldn't breathe." He spit on the ground. "One less piece of trash in the world."

Rowan might not have moved, but Rhetta could see his jaw harden, his fist tighten. He was hanging onto his rage by a thread.

"So, your wife killed my mother. Is that what you intend to do to me? Suffocate me with a pillow? Is that what happened to the sheriff who knew the truth? Who knew Ricky accidentally shot himself with the gun you gave him?"

"That nosy old sheriff got what he deserved," Mr. Reynolds said with a derisive snort. "After I strangled the life out of him, I tied a few bricks to the body and threw him in the river."

"Who else did you toss in the water?" Rowan asked.

Rhetta was sure he knew witnesses were listening to every word that was said.

Mr. Reynolds began rattling off a lengthy list before the senator turned and raised his pistol, pointing it at him. "Shut your mouth, Reynolds. You've said more than enough."

The man looked like he'd gladly bury a bullet in the senator's head if it wouldn't have ended what had been a lucrative career in crime.

"What you're saying, Pa," Rowan took a step back from the senator, "is that you've clawed and killed and cheated and lied to get to where you're at, and you don't regret a moment of it."

"It's politics, Reed. That's what you do to get ahead. If you'd been worth my time, I might have taught you that." He blinked a few times, like he was seeing Rowan for the first time. "You and

Ricky always looked so much alike, except you got your mother's gray eyes. His were brown. My Ricky's were brown."

Rowan moved another step back and lifted his hands in the air once again so no one could mistake his movements. "Why are you here, Pa? To shoot me? Or drag me back to Cincinnati so you can make a circus out of a mock trial and have someone with legal authority, someone you've likely bribed, sentence me to prison? Or is a hanging more your style?"

"Don't be crass. Hangings are messy and too public. I do have a few judges in my pocket I could ask to sentence you, but I don't want to ever see you again after today. I'm going to shoot you, then Mr. Reynolds is going to haul your worthless hide to the river and make sure you sink to the bottom, never to be seen again. But before I get to that, Miss Wallace might as well come out from wherever she's hiding. She's a sharp one, Reed. I had a feeling she knew more than she was saying from the start. Mr. Reynolds will make both her and her brat disappear."

"All nice and tidy, then you can return home the great hero, at least in your own warped mind." Rowan took one more step back. "I hate to tell you, Pa, but no one is dying today. Understand? No one."

The senator swung his gun around and pointed it in Rowan's face. "I'll shoot him right now, Miss Wallace, if you don't come out."

Rhetta handed the shotgun to the pastor.

"No, Mama! No!" Lee shouted in a whisper as he grabbed onto her shoulders.

She hugged him and spoke quietly. "You have to let me go, darling boy. Stay here and remember how much I love you."

Before anyone could stop her, she moved from behind the tree, holding her hands up in a defenseless position. "I'm right here, Senator. Rowan is correct, though. No one is dying today."

"That's what you think." Mr. Reynolds slid off his horse and pointed his gun at Rhetta as she walked over to Rowan. She moved until she stood so close to him, she could feel the heat pulsing off him in waves. Her legs felt like they might give way at any moment, but she tried to stand tall and proud, not letting the senator or Mr. Reynolds see how afraid she was.

"Where are the rest of your men?" Rhetta asked, looking around. "Surely, you two didn't come alone?"

Mr. Reynolds scowled. "I'm capable of handling you two on my own, but the boss wanted to see Reed one last time."

"To gloat over his victory?" Rhetta asked. "To once more attempt to convince himself his lies are real. What is the point? Why did you come, Senator?"

A twisted, evil grin filled the man's face. "So, I could watch the blood flow out of him, knowing he is no longer a taint on my life." The senator pulled back the hammer on his pistol just as the sound of guns cocking echoed all around them.

"Drop your weapons!" the marshal called as he rode into view from the other side of the senator and Mr. Reynolds. "Drop them and get on the ground. Now!"

Mr. Reynolds looked from the marshal to Rowan to his horse. He started to run for the animal, but a shot from the barn loft hit him in the thigh, and he fell to the ground, screaming in pain.

"Drop your weapon, Senator." Dillon rode over to the senator, pointing his rifle at his head. "You pull that trigger, and I'll pull mine. I'll hazard a guess I'm a far better shot than you are."

"I was merely defending myself, officer. This crazed cowhand and that trollop were weaving plots against me."

Dillon nodded to Josh Gatlin, who yanked the gun from the senator's hand and moved out of his reach. "I've been here the whole time, Senator. Heard every word you said. And I have half a dozen witnesses who will testify to everything you and Mr. Reynolds just stated to my friend Rowan. Seems to me you'd better get really cozy with the idea of spending the rest of your life in a jail cell."

"I need help! Get me a doctor," Mr. Reynolds whined.

"Evan?" Pastor Ryan yelled.

Rhetta couldn't hold back a laugh when the doctor stepped into view from where he'd taken a post up by Rowan's house.

"Want me to shoot him or get my doctor's bag?" Evan called.

"Up to you, Doc!" Dillon replied.

"I'll be right there," Evan said, holstering the gun he held in his hand.

"Did you deputize the whole town?" Rowan asked, grinning at Dillon.

"Only half of it. My wife said the women would ride in with guns blazing, so we left them at home."

The senator's eyes widened in shock. "What kind of depraved place is this?" he asked.

"The best kind of place, full of people who stand beside you when you most need them," Rowan said, catching the heavy handcuffs Dillon tossed to him and fastening them on his father's wrists. "This place is home."

The senator sneered at Rowan. "You're a mutt, Rowan. A cur. A worthless, useless, hopeless—"

The marshal's boot connected with the senator's mouth. His head snapped back, and he fell in an unconscious lump to the ground. "Whoops," Dillon said, with a feigned look of innocence.

"Aw, I missed it. Want to try that again with the other one?" R.C. asked as he jogged up to the group and reached for Mr. Reynolds.

"Keep that beast away from me," the man whimpered, scooting on the ground as he held his leg.

R.C. made a face and roared, pounding on his chest. Mr. Reynolds' eyes bulged right before he fainted. R.C. grinned at his friends. "Too bad Dillon couldn't show off that boot trick again."

Rowan latched onto Rhetta's right hand with his left, then walked around shaking hands with every man who was there. "I can't thank you all enough for coming. For caring. For helping. It takes a lot of courage to stand in the line of fire. If I can ever do the same for any of you, all you need to do is ask."

"Oh, we will, Rowan. You can count on it." R.C. thumped him on the shoulder, then helped dump the senator's and Mr. Reynolds' limp forms onto horses before the group headed back to town.

"Lee, come here," Rhetta said, when she saw her son standing with a hand on each of Rowan's dogs over by the tree where she'd hidden.

He ran over to them, and Rhetta hugged him. Rowan wrapped his arms around them both, holding them close as the dogs barked and ran around them. She sent up silent prayers of thanksgiving.

They were safe. They were together. And nothing would ever separate them again.

Chapter Twelve

"It's sure a pretty day for a wedding," Dillon commented as he stood with Rowan at the front of the church while they waited for Rhetta to appear and walk down the aisle.

Lee stood with them, tugging at his tie. "Is it straight?"

Rowan faced him and gave the tie a slight adjustment. "Just right." He started to reach out to ruffle the boy's hair, then stopped. Rhetta wouldn't like it if Lee's hair was mussed. She'd arranged for a photographer to come from Baker City to take their photos today. Rowan was determined everything be as close to perfect as possible for his bride.

He thought of the past few weeks and how the time had both dragged by and flown as he waited to wed Rhetta. She'd landed on a new career she could do from anywhere. With her talent at digging out the truth and facts, she'd been hired to write stories for a newspaper in Portland. She'd also sold a serial story to a newspaper in Cincinnati, covering the senator's downfall and deceit. Rowan was so proud of her, he might have busted the buttons right off his shirt, only that wouldn't bode well for the photographs she wanted.

"She's coming," Cora Lee Coleman whispered, then took a seat in the second pew at the church.

Grant Coleman had offered to walk Rhetta down the aisle, and she'd gladly accepted. She'd gone with a group of the women to Baker City to purchase a wedding gown and had accepted the offer of help with plans for the wedding.

Rowan had been glad to have assistance from his friends in adding two rooms to his house. It gave Lee his own bedroom, and it provided a private bedroom for Rowan and Rhetta on the other side of the house.

Jace Coleman had invited Lee to stay at Elk Creek Ranch while Rowan and Rhetta enjoyed a few days alone at their place.

Rowan had spent far too long this morning putting fresh sheets on the bed and filling every jar he could find with flowers he'd plucked from the abundance that bloomed around the original homestead foundation. Dillon's adopted grandmother, Nan, had put together a fragrant bouquet of flowers for Rhetta to carry.

Rowan watched Keeva Ryan and then Zara Durant walk down the aisle toward them before Grant and Rhetta came into view. His bride was a vision, with her gleaming hair piled on her head in loose waves with little white flowers woven into the style. She wore a gown in a deep blue hue that matched her eyes to perfection and carried the bouquet of white and yellow flowers from Nan. As Grant escorted her down the aisle, Rowan thought she couldn't look any prettier if she tried.

Dillon elbowed him, making Rowan grin. He knew what his friend was conveying. That life was good and sweet, and to cherish every moment of it.

Rowan had spent his whole life feeling like he wasn't good enough for anyone or anything. Now, he was marrying an incredible woman who loved him so much, she was willing to die beside him.

When he'd prayed for a partner in life, never expecting that prayer to be answered, he had no idea of the gift that awaited him in Rhetta. She was a gift to him, a blessing, and a treasure he would always cherish. Rhetta had given him dreams of hope and dreams for a future. Dreams for courage to never lose faith.

Grant winked at him as he placed Rhetta's hand on Rowan's. "You be good to this girl, or we'll all hunt you down."

Rowan nodded. "I promise to cherish her every day."

He heard Cora Lee sniffle and saw Jace pat her arm. She'd been crying all morning, and he had no idea why. The woman was generally not emotional, but she seemed to be exceedingly so today.

Rowan and Rhetta turned to face Pastor Ryan.

"Marriage is honorable among all men," the pastor said, smiling at them as he began the service.

Rowan was surprised he could peel his eyes away from Rhetta long enough to recite his vows. When it was time to kiss the bride, Rowan took a step closer to her and wrapped his hands around her waist. He lowered his head until their foreheads touched, and they stood there for a moment, basking in their joy and love. Then he used his index finger to push up her chin until their lips connected. He gave her a reverent, tender kiss before he pulled back and kissed both of her cheeks, then took her hand in his.

"Mr. and Mrs. Rowan Reed!" Dillon shouted, and the congregation broke into applause as Rowan rushed Rhetta down the aisle and out the door.

Outside, on the shady side of the church, tables and benches had been set up, where cake and punch were served.

Rowan glanced around the crowd, realizing he had truly found a home. A place where he was not only accepted but also welcomed, supported, and appreciated.

A home and a family, he amended, as he watched Rhetta stand with Lee, laughing at something Keeva said to her brother. Evan's face turned nearly as red as his hair, making them all laugh harder.

This town—and these people—were where he'd spent years trying to find. A place where he belonged and could love and be loved.

With deliberate steps, he walked over to Rhetta, slid his hand around her waist, and pulled her against him. His lips brushed her ear, and he felt a tremor slide over her. “Are you ready to go home, my love?”

“I’ve been ready since we said, ‘I do,’ husband. I love you. So very much.” Rhetta turned her head and kissed him lightly. “I will love you always, Rowan, with all my heart.”

“I will always love you, Rhetta, with all I am and hope to be. You and Lee, and whatever children we may have will always be my home.”

“And that’s why I adore you, Rowan Reed. Because you have a heart as huge as that big, beautiful body of yours.”

He gave her a wicked grin and swung her into his arms, earning cheers and applause from their friends as he carried her out to the buggy R.C. was letting them borrow. “What do you know about my big body?”

“That what I saw the first day I came out to the ranch when you didn’t have on a shirt was deliciously attractive, even if you were positively indecent.”

“Doesn’t matter now, does it?” Rowan asked, setting her in the buggy, then kissing her soundly.

“What matters?” she asked, appearing dazed by his kiss.

“Nothing. Not a thing, but how much I love you, Rhetta. Today, tomorrow, and always.”

“Always. I like the sound of that.” She wrapped her hands around his arm as he snapped the lines and they started away from the church and into their future. A future they would face with courage, hope, and abiding love.

Strawberry Pie Recipe

Although this isn't exactly like the pie Rhetta, Rowan, and Lee enjoyed on their picnic, it's a modern version of a tasty treat!

Strawberry Pie

INGREDIENTS

For the Crust:

1 cup graham cracker crumbs
¾ cup coarsely chopped pretzels
3 tablespoons granulated sugar
½ cup butter, melted

For the Filling:

3 pounds fresh strawberries
1 cup granulated sugar
⅓ cup boiling water
3 tablespoons cornstarch
1 teaspoon vanilla extract

DIRECTIONS

In a medium bowl, stir together graham cracker crumbs, chopped pretzels, and sugar. Stir in the melted butter until well combined. Press into the bottom and up the sides (about ½ inch) of a greased 9-inch springform pan. Set in the refrigerator to chill while preparing the filling.

Wash the berries, remove tops, and place 2 cups of berries into the bowl of a food processor or a blender and puree. Add sugar, boiling water, and cornstarch, then blend until smooth.

Pour the mixture into a medium saucepan and bring to a boil over medium heat, stirring constantly. Once it boils, continue boiling (and stirring) for three minutes. The mixture will get thick and less cloudy as it cooks. Remove from heat, stir in vanilla, and set aside to cool.

Cut the remaining strawberries into slices or bite-sized pieces. Stir the cut strawberries into the glaze, then spoon into the crust. Chill the pie for at least two hours.

Yield: approximately 8 slices

Author's Note

Thank you for coming along on another Holiday Dreams adventure. I hope you enjoyed Rowan and Rhetta's romance. I so enjoyed writing about their journey to their happily ever after.

When I was thinking about the perfect heroine for Rowan since we first met him in *Dreams of Love*, I wanted a strong, independent woman who had an unusual career.

That's when I landed on the idea of making her a private detective. Apparently, there were many women working in that profession in the 1800s although it was rare for them to own their own agency, like Rhetta. I even happened across some advertisements from female private detectives. One of them stated: "*Ladies - when in need of legal or confidential advice why not confer with one of your own sex?*" Direct. To the point. Just like our Rhetta.

When I had Rowan out cutting grass with a scythe, I so well remembered doing that down in a gully where the ground was too boggy for the tractor to get into to cut the grass. On a muggy summer day when the air felt stifling and suffocating, I was swinging a scythe back and forth with some degree of care, my mother's admonitions not to whack my leg off ringing in my ears. I managed not to whack off my leg or electrocute myself on the electric fence under which I was cutting away the overgrown grass. I remember the feel of the scythe in my hands on that hot summer day and could relate to Rowan as he worked. Thank goodness for modern farm equipment!

When I was searching through old newspapers for something fun to include in the story, I was delighted to come across an article in the June 11, 1886 issue of "The Oregon Statesmen" about Grover Cleveland's wedding to Frances Folsom. He was 49, and she was just 21 when they exchanged vows June 2, 1886, in the Blue Room at the White House. She became the youngest First Lady, and Cleveland was the first and only president to be married in the White House while in office.

I could just imagine the excitement the article would stir in the female readers of the newspaper and could so vividly picture Anne and Cora Lee animatedly discussing the wedding, the fashions, and how romantic the whole thing had to be.

Weddings are generally such a fun topic to incorporate into my stories. I'm glad I could share Rowan and Rhetta's with you.

Do you have any characters from Holiday you'd like to see have their own story? If so, please let me know.

My deep thanks to Katrina, Allison, Linda, and my Hopeless Romantics team for helping make this book the best possible version it could be.

Until we meet between the pages of another book, happy reading!

Shanna

Preview Love on Target

Eastern Oregon
April 1894

"We're almost somewhere, Scout." Rena Burke patted the neck of her faithful mule as she stared between the slats of the stock car where she traveled on a rocking train bound for Portland, Oregon.

She'd argued with the stationmaster back in Colorado until she'd given herself a headache about riding with Scout instead of taking a seat in a passenger car. When she'd refused to defer to his commands, the man must have realized it was pointless to tell her otherwise. He'd finally relented and allowed her to stay with her mule. Once he'd elicited her promise to remain in the stock car, the stationmaster had given her a discounted fare.

If Scout hadn't been worn out past endurance after carrying her from Amarillo to Denver, she wouldn't have splurged on the expense of boarding the train. However, it wasn't just Scout's weary state that had compelled her to pay the fare. Weeks of traveling alone coupled with a handful of frightening encounters along the way due to beasts with four legs, as well as some with two, had removed any doubt about continuing the trip on a train.

The last thing Rena wanted was to sit among people who gave her curious glances or disapproving glares. Just because she chose to wear trousers and her father's old brown hat didn't mean people should automatically judge her. Then again, the stares might be aimed at her because of the limp she couldn't hide no matter how hard she tried.

Thoughts of life before she'd acquired the limp made her maudlin, so she returned her attention to watching out of the stock car slats as the train entered what appeared to be a prosperous town. She'd fallen asleep last night after dark and had only awakened an hour ago. Dawn was just beginning to stretch across the sky, but it was light enough she could see houses, businesses, and wide streets as the train screeched to a stop.

She heard someone, presumably the conductor, raise his voice above the racket. "Welcome to Baker City, folks. Welcome to the queen city of the Inland Empire!"

At least the man's loud announcement assured Rena she had arrived at her destination to disembark the train. She brushed straw from her clothes and hastily braided her hair before settling the hat on her head. She saddled Scout, adjusted the saddlebags, and hung another bag of her belongings from the saddle horn. The reins dangled from her left hand as she waited for the door to open.

Part of the trip, she and Scout had shared the stock car with a mare with no manners and a gelding that had appeared half-starved. Rena had fed the gelding a portion of the feed she'd purchased for Scout. Both horses had been led off the train yesterday afternoon, and no more had been brought to their car.

Thankful for the reprieve from being around other animals and humans, Rena had been able to relax last night and get a good night's rest. She figured she'd need all her strength as she continued on her journey.

Finally, the door to the stock car opened. Two men in denim overalls slid a wooden ramp into place, and she walked down it with Scout's breath blowing warmth against her back.

"Come on, boy," she said softly, stepping out into a morning that bore a fresh, pleasant scent, along with the aroma of bacon and coffee. Her stomach rumbled in hunger, but she ignored it as she held her head high, kept her posture stiff, and led Scout away from the depot.

Rena could have boarded another train for the last segment of her trip, but she wanted to take in the surroundings of the place that was to be her new home. She didn't want her first view of Holiday, Oregon, to be from inside the stock car.

Rather than immediately leave Baker City, she wandered through town, stopping outside a mercantile. She would need a few provisions to see her through another night or two on the trail.

Rena looped Scout's reins around a hitching rail, leaned against it, and waited for the store to open. As the sun rose, it carried welcome heat. She tipped her hat and head back until the warm rays of the golden orb caressed her face.

Footsteps behind her drew her from her brief yet peaceful interlude. She opened her eyes and turned around to be greeted by a friendly shopkeeper with a welcoming smile.

"Morning. You waiting to get in?" the man asked, keys dangling from a leather string held between his fingers as he stood near the door.

"Yes, sir. I just need to pick up a few things before I head out." Rena pushed away from the rail and followed him inside a well-stocked store. She breathed in the scents of leather, spices, and kerosene.

"Feel free to look around. I'm Frank Miller, owner of the mercantile." He held his hand out to her in greeting.

"Nice to meet you, Mr. Miller. Rena Burke. I'm heading up to Holiday." She shook his hand, then stepped back. "My cousin lives there."

"It's a pretty little town, up in the mountains like it is. Have you been there before?"

Rena shook her head. "No, sir. What's the best way to get there?"

He quirked a bushy eyebrow. "On Hope."

"Hope?" she asked while doing her best to swallow her annoyance. Hope was a fine thing to have, but her well of hope had run dry two years ago. It sure wouldn't give her feet wings and fly her and Scout to Holiday. In fact, she was certain the One who gave hope had all but forgotten about her.

Mr. Miller grinned. "Hope is the name of the engine that pulls the Holiday Express train up the mountain. Everyone around these parts refers to the train as Hope."

"I see. I, uh … won't be riding the train." Or riding hope off into the sunset, for that matter. She'd learned the hard way the only person she could depend on was herself, not some fanciful notion that anyone would help her when she needed it most. "What's the next best way to get to Holiday?"

"There's a wagon road. You'll head east out of town, then northwest a few miles before the trail swings around to the north. There are a few signs posted along the way. You can't miss it if you stay on the road."

"How long would it take to get there, do you reckon?" Rena fingered a book from a shelf filled with interesting titles. It had been ages since she'd had anything new to read, but she wouldn't waste any of her precious pennies on the luxury of a book. Her cousin had a collection of books. She was sure she'd find plenty of reading material at his place.

"If you're planning to ride that ol' mule tied out there to the hitching rail, I'd say it will take you a day and a half, maybe two. The elevation gets higher as you go, and you don't want to push him too hard. There are a few smaller towns along the way. I'd recommend spending the night in one of them. The church in Aldeen, which also serves as the school, would be a good place for a person to get in out of the dark and cold if they didn't have other options. There's a little shed out back where the teacher leaves her horse and buggy during school hours. As long as you didn't disturb anything, no one would care if you stayed there."

"That's good to know. Thank you."

While Mr. Miller stoked the pot-bellied stove and made a pot of coffee, Rena browsed around the store. Her gaze lingered on a bolt of brocade peach taffeta. She hadn't worn a dress in two years, and none that she'd owned had been created from such costly, beautiful fabric. A girl like her had no business dreaming about expensive things. It wouldn't matter how she dressed, anyway. Not now. She could look like a queen, and it wouldn't do her a bit of good.

No man would ever want her, and she'd arrived at the point she no longer cared. Who needed love with all the anxiety and heartache that went along with it?

Rena had gotten along well enough on her own. The thought of a man bossing her around, telling her what to do and when to do it, made her balk at the very notion of it. She preferred to remain alone and independent than relinquish her freedom.

Which was precisely the reason she was heading to Holiday to see her cousin. She held high hopes she could start over there without the past dogging her every faltering step. Theo had even hinted in his last letter that he might have a job lined up for her at the mine where he worked.

Rena filled a tin with crackers from the barrel in the store. When she took the crackers to the front counter, Mr. Miller handed her a cup of hot coffee that was the best thing she'd tasted since she'd left Amarillo. While he cut the wedge of cheese she'd requested, Rena sipped the strong, black brew and looked through a display of gloves. A pair of work gloves, made of the softest leather, fit her hands to perfection. She dearly wanted the gloves, but the price forced her to return them to the shelf.

As she finished the cup of coffee, she added dried apples, a tablet with a pencil, and a sack of assorted penny candy to her purchases.

"Is there a place in town where I could buy feed for my mule? I don't want to start up the mountain before he's properly fed and watered."

"Sure. Head over to Milt's Livery. He's honest and fair and will take good care of your mule. If you're looking for a meal, the bakery should be open by now, or there are a few restaurants, but you'll get more food for less expense at the bakery. You could go there while Milt sees to your mule."

Rena nodded, hoping Mr. Miller couldn't hear the gnawing roar of hunger in her empty belly. She'd run out of food yesterday morning and decided she could do without until they arrived in Baker City. Now that they were here, she really should get something to eat, or she might be too weak to journey onward.

When the store owner gave her the total for her purchases, she took money from her pocket and counted it out to the penny.

"I hope you have a safe trip to Holiday, Miss Burke. Just be sure you don't travel at night. There are bears in the mountains and cougars in the hills, not to mention a few unsavory types who wouldn't be above waylaying anyone they see traveling alone."

Surprised by his words of caution, she intended to heed his warning. Old Scout wouldn't stand a chance against a bear or cougar. The crotchety fella was half afraid of cats as it was. Rena could shoot anyone who bothered her, but she'd rather not get into a situation where defending herself was necessary.

"It was nice to meet you, Mr. Miller." She nodded to him in gratitude. "Thank you for the advice and the coffee."

"You're welcome. Come back anytime." Mr. Miller waved as she carried her purchases outside, stowed them in her saddlebags, and then led Scout up the street in the direction the store owner had indicated she'd find the livery.

She crossed a side street and saw the sign for the livery just ahead.

"Morning," a beefy-armed man said as she stepped inside. "Can I help you with something?"

"I was hoping to buy a little feed for my mule and give him a place to rest for about an hour." Rena glanced around the livery as her eyes adjusted from being out in the sunlight to the darker interior that smelled of hay and horses. At a glance, the place appeared clean and orderly, showing the owner took pride in the upkeep of his business. Assured she was about to leave Scout in good hands, she loosened her tight grip on the reins.

"I'd be happy to help you with that, miss." He told her what he'd charge, then motioned toward an empty stall. "I about forgot my manners, miss. I'm Milt Owens, and this is my livery. Haven't seen you around Baker City before."

"I'm just passing through," Rena said, leading Scout into a stall that had fresh straw on the floor and a bucket full of clear water. Scout sniffed the water, then took a long drink.

"Where you heading?" Mr. Owens asked as he filled a shallow pan with feed and set it inside the stall. Scout didn't waste any time in tasting it.

Rena ignored his question and motioned to her mule. "Thank you for seeing to Scout, sir."

"My pleasure." He jabbed his thumb over his shoulder toward the door. "If you need a meal, I recommend the bakery. They have the best cinnamon buns I've ever tasted."

"I'll do that, Mr. Owens. Mr. Miller at the mercantile also recommended the bakery. Thank you again for keeping an eye on Scout." Rena hated to be apart from Scout, but she was starving. The mention of cinnamon buns made her mouth water. At the rate she was going, she'd start to slobber, and someone would assume she'd gone rabid and threaten to put her out of her misery.

Before she changed her mind, she nodded once to Mr. Owens, marched out the door, and headed back in the direction she'd come. She turned at the corner and pulled up short before she plowed right over one of the most fashionable women she'd ever seen. Thick, dark hair was stylishly arranged beneath a hat that matched a glorious gown in a deep shade of raspberry pink. The woman's skin was flawless, her eyes bright, and her smile wide as she studied Rena.

"Good morning," the woman spoke in a soft, friendly tone.

"Good morning," Rena said, wishing she could look even a smidgen as elegant as the woman. "I apologize for not watching where I was going."

Much to her dismay and mortification, Rena's stomach chose that moment to rumble loudly. The heat of embarrassment seared her cheeks. She had to force herself not to duck her head and run off.

The woman's smile widened. "Were you on your way to the bakery, by chance?"

"I was. Mr. Miller at the mercantile and Mr. Owens at the livery both recommended it."

"I'll walk with you." The woman looped her arm around Rena's. "My husband was going to pick up some pastries for our breakfast and meet me at my shop. I'm Maggie MacGregor."

"It's nice to meet you, Mrs. MacGregor. I'm Rena Burke. You own a business in town?" Rena asked, taken aback by the notion of such a lovely woman managing a business.

"I own and manage the dress shop here in town. It brings me great satisfaction to create gowns that people seem to love wearing. I also sell ready-made clothing as well as hats, stockings, gloves, and some attire for children."

Rena glanced down at her dusty trousers, a shirt that had been clean a week ago, and the baggy jacket that had once belonged to her father. It was a wonder Mrs. MacGregor hadn't taken one look at her and hastened in the other direction.

"Are you traveling, Miss Burke?"

Rena nodded, trying not to gawk as they strolled down a street that was brimming with early morning activity. A man in a duster with a bronze star pinned to the front waved and touched his fingers to the brim of his hat from across the street as he spoke with two cowboys.

"That's Tully Barrett, the sheriff. We've been friends for what seems like forever." Mrs. MacGregor returned his wave, then gestured toward a park. "Will you be in town long? Our park is quite glorious when all the trees and flowers are in bloom."

"I plan to leave in about an hour," Rena said, standing on a corner waiting for two wagons to pass. "What does your husband do, Mrs. MacGregor?"

"Ian owns the lumberyard. It's a constant battle to keep sawdust out of the carpets," she said with a laugh, then playfully bumped her shoulder against Rena's arm. "Please, call me Maggie."

"I'll do that if you call me Rena."

Maggie smiled at her again. "Where are you from and what direction are you heading?"

"I'm from Amarillo, Texas, and I'm heading up to Holiday to see my cousin. He bought some land up there last year. Theo offered to let me stay with him awhile, so here I am."

"Gracious! Did you travel all that way alone?" Maggie questioned as they crossed the street and moved into the line that stretched outside the bakery door.

"I had my mule with me. He's the closest thing I have to a friend."

Maggie frowned. "Well, now you have two. Anytime you come to Baker City, I hope you'll stop by my shop. It's right on the main street that runs through town, not far from the hotel."

Rena couldn't envision herself in a dress shop, but she nodded to be polite. "I'll do that, Maggie. Thank you for the invitation and the offer of friendship."

"Of course." Maggie leaned around the people in front of them and motioned to someone near the front of the line, held up three fingers and pointed to Rena, then tugged her out of line.

"Ian will get enough for all three of us. Let's go sit on a bench across the street. The one right there by the maple tree is the best spot to soak up the morning light."

Without waiting for Rena's reply, Maggie glided across the street and gracefully settled her skirts around her as she took a seat on a wooden bench.

Rena felt like a filthy pauper next to Maggie, but before she could think of a reason to excuse herself, a handsome man with blond hair and lively blue eyes strode across the street, holding a box in one hand and three cups of something hot that steamed in the crisp morning air in the other.

"Well, hello," he said with the faintest hint of a brogue as he greeted her with a broad smile. "I see my Maggie has coerced you into eating breakfast with us. I'm Ian."

"It's nice to meet you, Mr. MacGregor," Rena said, standing as he set the box beside Maggie, handed his wife one of the cups, then kissed her cheek.

He handed Rena a cup, then politely bowed his head to her. "Call me Ian. And you are?"

"Rena. Rena Burke. I'm just passing through town and left my mule with Mr. Owens at the livery while I got a little something to eat. As soon as we've both had breakfast, we'll be on our way."

"To Holiday," Maggie said, lifting a plate with a large bun from the box and handing it to Rena. "There are some lovely, lovely people who live there. If you meet the Coleman or Milton families, please give them my regards."

"I'll do that," Rena said, accepting the plate from Maggie.

Ian motioned for her to take a seat on the bench as he lifted a plate holding a huge cinnamon bun from the box, then propped one booted foot on the bench by Maggie.

Rena settled on the bench and took a tentative sip from the cup that warmed her chilled hands. The coffee was even better than the pot Mr. Miller had made. She took another sip before she set the cup on the bench beside her and lifted her fork. Maggie and Ian bowed their heads, and Ian asked a brief blessing on their meal.

Out of long-ingrained habit, Rena bowed her head and said, "amen." She hadn't prayed in two years, but today wasn't the day to examine the reasons why.

Instead, she forked a bite of the cinnamon bun still warm from the oven with gooey icing dripping off the sides. She closed her eyes to better enjoy her second bite.

As they ate, Ian and Maggie filled the quiet, talking about Baker City and Holiday, and encouraging her to seek them out if she returned to town.

When they finished their simple meal, Rena tried to pay Ian, but he shook his head.

"It was our pleasure, Rena, to share breakfast with a new friend."

Maggie gathered the dishes into the box Ian had carried, and he picked it up with one hand. "I'd better get these back to the bakery before they think I've absconded with them. 'Twas a wonderful, unexpected gift to meet you this morning, Rena. Safe travels to you." He kissed Maggie's cheek. "Wait a moment, my lovely lass, and I'll walk you to the shop."

Maggie stood as Ian rushed back across the street with the dishes, then shifted her focus to Rena. "Are you sure you wouldn't like to stay in town for a while?"

"No. I really need to be on my way, but thank you for your kindness and for breakfast. Are you certain I can't pay for my meal?"

"Absolutely certain. It was a treat for us to share breakfast with you."

Rena saw no need to prolong her goodbye. She highly doubted she'd ever see Ian and Maggie again anyway. "I'm thankful I got to meet you both. If you ever venture up to Holiday, let me know. My cousin's name is Theo Marshall."

"If we get up that way, we'll definitely plan to say hello."

Maggie squeezed Rena's hand and gave her a thoughtful look before she let go. "Be safe, Rena."

"I will." Rena spun around and cut through the park on her way back to the livery. She didn't know what it was about meeting the friendly, sweet couple, but observing the loving looks they shared made her want to cry.

And Rena never cried.

Ranted, yes.

Brooded, often.

But cried?

Not for a long, long time.

She drew in a deep lungful of air and rushed back to the livery.

Mr. Owens was speaking softly to Scout and patting him on the neck when she marched inside the building.

"There you are. I was just telling Scout you'd be back any minute. He cleaned up every bite of his breakfast and drank a good share of the water. Are you heading a far distance today?"

"Aldeen, I think," Rena said, putting the worn-out bridle Mr. Owens had removed back on Scout. She'd already decided she'd spend the night in the church in Aldeen. From what Mr. Miller had shared, it seemed like her safest, and least costly, option.

"That's a fair piece to travel. Do you have a gun or know how to shoot it?"

Rena nodded. "I do." She'd stowed her gun belt in one of the saddlebags while she'd slept last night and hadn't put it back on. Now, she pulled it out and fastened it around her hips. It had belonged to her father, and Rena had practiced shooting it until she rarely missed her mark.

Unable to help herself, Rena took the pistol from the holster and spun it around on her finger a few times, holstering it again in a matter of seconds.

Mr. Owens gaped at her with wide eyes, then he grinned. "You're a regular Annie Oakley, Miss Burke. I reckon you can handle yourself. You do any fancy shooting with that rifle you have in the scabbard?"

His reference to Annie Oakley delighted Rena beyond words. Although she'd never had the opportunity to watch Annie Oakley perform, she'd read every newspaper account she could find about the woman who had become her inspiration and something of a heroine to Rena. Annie had validated

Rena's notion that women could step beyond the roles assigned to them by society and succeed at whatever they chose to pursue.

"Sometimes, Mr. Owens." She offered the livery owner a pleased smile. "Thanks again for taking care of Scout." She paid him, led the mule outside, and swung into the saddle.

"Safe travels." Mr. Owens lifted his hand in departure as she clucked her tongue against her cheek, and Scout began a slow mosey down the street.

Rena glanced over her shoulder and tipped her head to the livery owner, then focused her gaze ahead. She'd found there was no purpose in looking back. None at all. Most of the time, there was no one who cared if she left, anyway.

The following afternoon, she heard the whistle of the train as it rolled into Holiday at nearly the same time she and Scout arrived in the town that would become her new home. Although the trip up the mountain had been uneventful, she was relieved to reach Holiday.

Last night, she'd arrived in Aldeen just before dusk and tracked down the pastor to get his permission to stay in the church, or school, whichever one wanted to call it. He'd invited her to join him and his wife for dinner, which she'd accepted. When they'd insisted that she spend the night with them, she gently refused but thanked them for the meal and the opportunity to sleep somewhere safe and warm.

After Rena had settled Scout in the lean-to the teacher used for her horse and given him a portion of feed and a bucket of fresh water, she'd bedded down on a blanket on a pew in the church, staring at the shadowed ceiling before sleep had finally claimed her.

She'd awakened at four that morning and ridden out of town a few minutes later. The early start was the only reason she'd made it to Holiday before dark. Scout seemed as anxious as she felt to reach their destination.

Holiday appeared to be a growing, busy town. The wide main street was a beehive of activity with wagons coming and going. She saw two wagons full of lumber rumble by and wondered if Ian ever shipped lumber up to Holiday. Likely not. Theo had mentioned a lumber mill located near some of the mines.

As she entered the outskirts of town, Rena rode past a beautiful home set back from the road with a broad porch that looked inviting. Across the pasture from it, she passed a livery and blacksmith shop.

Further up the street, a sign painted on a window proclaimed the camel-colored building to be the assay office.

Next door, a little girl with a mop of blonde curls stood on top of a saddle in the window of the saddle shop. She held a doll in one hand and waved at Rena with the other.

Rena smiled and returned the tiny fairylike child's wave, then fixed her attention on the town of Holiday. Across the side street from the saddle shop was a large hotel with a restaurant sign. The smell of roasting meat made her wish she'd purchased more food yesterday. She'd eaten the last bite of cheese and the remnants of broken crackers hours ago when she'd stopped for a rest at lunch.

She made note of the mercantile, a post office, and a dress shop. The colorful frocks in the window made her think of Ian and Maggie. Rena felt a sense of gratification in knowing if she ever did return to

Baker City, she had two friends there who might be pleased to see her.

The sight of the church made Rena look the other way, taking in the stage office, marshal's office, and the jail instead. She rode on the main street until she reached the other end of town and continued north.

Theo had written that his place was a few miles from town on the east side of the road. He'd told her to ride around a curve in the road, then look for a stump that was shaped like a chair. His cabin—or shack, as he called it—was a hundred yards back in the trees.

Rena removed her hat and tilted her face up to the sun as she traveled along on Scout's swayed back, breathing in the lush mountain air. She could grow accustomed to the scent of the breeze that carried a hint of pine and smelled like Christmastime.

The peacefulness surrounding her calmed her jittery nerves at seeing Theo again after so many years apart. He had already left home to pursue his own adventures before her world had fallen apart. However, he and his sister, Laura, had always been close to her, more like siblings than cousins. As an only child, Rena had cherished time spent with them when they were younger, even if they'd all traveled different paths as adults.

When Rena happened upon a stump that did indeed look like someone had roughly hacked out chunks of it until it resembled a chair, she turned and rode along a path through the trees.

At the edge of a meadow, she found a weathered cabin she assumed had to be Theo's home. She stopped Scout near the door, grateful to see a barn that would keep wild critters away from the mule. From the straight lines of it and the fresh coat of red paint, she assumed Theo had built it after purchasing the land last year.

As she swung out of the saddle, she cocked an ear, listening to the sound of water. There must be a creek nearby. If Theo didn't have a well, a creek would be a handy thing to have on his place.

She tied Scout's reins around a half-rotten post that was sunken into the ground, patted his neck, then strode to the door. Rena lifted her hand and knocked twice, waited, then knocked two more times. When no one answered, she tried the knob. It turned in her hand, so she pushed open the door.

"Hello? Anyone home? Hello?" Hesitant to intrude in case it wasn't Theo's home, Rena cautiously stepped inside. Her gaze followed the dust motes dancing in a beam of sunlight streaming in the window by the door. A table covered by a checkered cloth sat beneath the window. An oil lamp, a stack of books, and a glass sugar bowl with a lid on top rested in the center of the table.

"Hello? Theo?" Rena moved further into the room, taking in the simple furnishings.

The cabin was all one big room. At the far end was a fireplace and to the right of it, a cookstove. A coffee pot on the top of the stove made her long for a cup. There'd be time enough to make a pot later.

A sink with a pump handle to draw water and a small window above it were on the same side of the room as the stove. Two wooden crates with shelves built into them were fastened to the wall on either side of the sink. One held an assortment of dishes. The other crate held tins and jars that appeared to contain spices.

A large bed took up the space to the left of the fireplace. Pegs held a few shirts, a heavy wool coat, and a black hat. On the floor beneath the pegs were a pair of newer-looking boots. Another oil lamp sat on a trunk pushed into the corner that appeared to serve as an end table. The only other piece of furniture on that side of the cabin was a small chest of drawers.

On the opposite end of the cabin were two rocking chairs and another table, this one strewn with papers. A ladder nailed to the wall went up to an open loft area. By stepping into the doorway and tipping back her head, Rena could see a bed in the loft covered by a colorful quilt.

She walked across the room to a bookcase, made of rough lumber, that held numerous books, interesting rocks, and keepsakes. A small wooden box that had once belonged to her aunt brought sweet memories to mind. The letter "M" engraved on the outside of it was unmistakable. Rena opened the lid to see a stack of letters. One she'd written to Theo before she'd left Amarillo rested on top.

Even if her cousin wasn't at home, at least she was in the right place. Relieved she wasn't poking around a stranger's home, Rena returned outside. She led Scout to the barn and settled him in a stall with feed and a bucket of water she filled from the pump she'd found near the barn.

Exhaustion overtook her as she carried her bags and rifle inside the cabin. The only thing she could think of at that moment was rest, but she was filthy. She set her bags on the floor, propped the rifle behind the door, and removed her hat and gun belt, hanging them on a peg behind the door. She then retrieved a clean shirt and pair of trousers. Although they were wrinkled, at least they didn't smell like sweat, dirt, and mule.

She rummaged through her things and retrieved a comb and bar of soap, then searched the cabin. Towels were stacked on a shelf near the bed. Rena took her pistol from the holster, then carried everything outside and followed the sound of water to the creek.

After looking around to ensure she was alone, she removed her filthy clothes and rolled them together in a bundle, left her pistol on top of them, and stepped into the chilly water that moved with a rapid current. The first feel of the frigid water against her skin made her want to jump right back out, but instead, she waded into the middle of the creek where it came up past her knees, sat down, and scrubbed away miles and days of dirt. She washed her hair and shook away the droplets, then returned to the bank where she wrapped one towel around her and the other around her head. Briskly rubbing her skin dry, she hastily dressed, then combed the tangles from her hair. She sat on a large rock in a pool of sunshine that spilled through the trees, closed her eyes, and immediately fell asleep.

Available on Amazon

Thank You

Thank you for reading *Dreams For Courage.* If you enjoyed the story, I'd be so grateful if you would leave a review. It's a great way for readers to discover new-to-them authors!

Be sure you check out all the books in the Holiday Dreams series!

About the Author

PHOTO BY SHANA BAILEY PHOTOGRAPHY

USA Today bestselling author Shanna Hatfield is a farm girl who loves to write. Her sweet historical and contemporary romances are filled with sarcasm, humor, hope, and hunky heroes.

When Shanna isn't dreaming up unforgettable characters, twisting plots, or covertly seeking dark, decadent chocolate, she hangs out with her beloved husband, Captain Cavedweller, at their home in the Pacific Northwest.

Shanna loves to hear from readers.

Connect with her online:

Website: shannahatfield.com

Email: shanna@shannahatfield.com

Printed in Great Britain
by Amazon

45549840R00108